Edward Farmer

Ned Farmer's Scrap Book

Being a Selection of Poems, Songs, Scraps, etc. etc.

Edward Farmer

Ned Farmer's Scrap Book
Being a Selection of Poems, Songs, Scraps, etc. etc.

ISBN/EAN: 9783337179120

Printed in Europe, USA, Canada, Australia, Japan

Cover: Foto ©Andreas Hilbeck / pixelio.de

More available books at **www.hansebooks.com**

BEING A SELECTION OF

POEMS, SONGS, SCRAPS,

ETC. ETC.

ENLARGED AND REVISED.

"NONSENSE PRECIPITATE, LIKE RUNNING LEAD,
THAT SLIPP'D THRO' CRACKS AND ZIGZAGS OF THE HEAD." *Pope.*

THIRD EDITION.

LONDON
W. MACINTOSH, 24, PATERNOSTER ROW

DERBY
BEMROSE & SONS, IRONGATE AND MARKET-PLACE
1863.

PRINTED AND PUBLISHED FOR THE AUTHOR,
BY BEMROSE & SONS, IRONGATE AND MARKET-PLACE, DERBY

PREFACE.

In the year 1846, I had the temerity to publish a small
yea, a VERY small—collection of Poems, Songs, Scraps, &c.,
then, as now, under the title of "Ned Farmer's Scrap
Book;" all of which, as the immortal Sairey Gamp would
say, "is well beknown." The very kind manner in which
the diminutive tome alluded to, was received by my friend,
and the amiable forbearance evinced by the few reviewers
who condescended to notice it, have mainly actuated me in
thus daring again to meet the public gaze. Further than
this, it may just be, as is often the case, the few have
brought the infliction on the many; for, travelling as I do
very much, I have often been asked, whether in jest or
earnest the inquirers best know, where my Scrap Book could
be obtained : and being induced to look over " the nooks
and corners of old England "—meaning my boxes, drawers,
writing-desk, &c.— I discovered among many other queer
crudities of the brain, the varied contents of the little work
now offered, with the most profound respect, for general
perusal ; the chameleon-like nature of which will go to
prove under what varied moods and feelings they have
had their birth.

> For I am one who only writes,
> Just when the "mental machine" likes

But, argues Common Sense, admitting all this to be true
why not be content, as scores of far better writers have

been, to keep within the healthy compass of unpretending manuscript, this " mad material of the mind ?"   To all such inquiry, albeit most judiciously and forcibly put, I merely reply, " What should I get by that ?"

Again, if BETTER writers than myself are deterred by prudential, or other and worthier motives, from publishing " their brilliant corruscations," must it not be clearly in favour of myself and " such small deer," who have had the bad taste to trouble a publisher ?   Why, I say Yes to that.

Well, well, a wilful man must have his way, says the old adage ; and were it not so, this, the Third Edition of " Ned Farmer's Scrap Book " had never met the enraptured gaze of an admiring world !   (Rather fine writing that, I flatter myself.)   For it is simply wonderful what an amount of trouble some of my quondam friends and acquaintances have been at in endeavouring to dissuade me from what they, in the exuberance of their zeal, have kindly designated "making a fool of myself."   Well, *nous verrons.*

Others there are, who, as a deterrent, have narrated for my special behoof, a list of glorious names, among whom were enumerated such giants of the pen as Robert Burns, Tom Moore, and—though last, not least in our dear love, -" Tom Hood ;" and, putting it to me in tones of mingled contempt and derision, if I really had the astounding impudence to dare—aye, marry, dare was the word—to publish the lame and limping offspring of my muse, in the same country, and in the same language.   To all of which I give for answer, one loud, emphatic Yes !

Why, what on earth have I, poor poetaster as I am, to do with those proud names, or the myriads of mental diamonds

which they in their abundance have scattered broadcast
o'er the land, beyond the high, and I trust duly appreciated
privilege of being permitted to peruse those bright undying
records of their genius — the works they left us ?

Again, is it by any means an unusual circumstance, that
a dwarf and a giant are exhibited in the same town,
nay, sometimes in the selfsame caravan ? Is my simple fife
to be unheard because other and better performers play
upon ophicleides and trombones ? Am I not to vend my
sprats, because, forsooth, there happens to be salmon in the
market ? Because I possess not the fleetness of a Deerfoot,
am I therefore to sit ingloriously still ? Nonsense ! in mild
and subdued tones, but with a decided amount of firmness,
I repeat, Nonsense !

Do me, O courteous Reader, I conjure ye, the justice to
believe me, when I most solemnly assert that, in bringing
out the Third Edition of my Scrap Book, I was perfectly
free from any wild and ambitious expectancies as to what
was likely to accrue therefrom. I anticipated no proud niche
in Westminster Abbey ; and, as "I am a tall man and a
gentleman," I never for a single moment had it in my mind
to thrust from his well-filled throne the Poet Laureate, or
snatch from his magic hand the well-earned sceptre he so
worthily grasps. I had no futile hope of thereby immortal-
izing the humble name I bear ; I entertained no insane idea
of amassing a colossal fortune.

Beyond this I feel bound to state, that no person breath
ing, can by any possibility be more thoroughly alive to the
numberless shortcomings and defects of my Scrap Book than
myself ; but what was I to do ? People would keep asking

for it.   I had a lot of pieces of one kind or other stowed
away, and lying about in drawers, cupboards, and boxes, and
it was quite a certainty that if I did not publish them, no one
else ever would; and it just became a question with me,
whether I should burn them or print them.   I decided on
the latter course, and *hinc illæ lachrymæ*.

This also did I take into account : that having, miserable
varlet as I am, no fond and devoted wife to be pained by the
eccentricities of her husband—no loving children (the more
of misery mine) to be taunted with their father's follies—I
decided upon the present course of action ; and, as a friend
of mine would say, " I've been and gone and done it ! "

Had I more of time than my present avocation allows me,
I am free to confess that I would have endeavoured to
have licked into somewhat better shape these rough and
uncouth "bear cubs" of my brain.   True it is, that more
than one kindly-disposed individual has volunteered to
parse and otherwise alter and amend the varied contents
of my book ; but such offers I have ever declined firmly,
yet, I trust, respectfully : for had I permitted such alter-
ations as doubtless better taste and higher learning had
suggested, the book would have ceased to have been my
production, and would have been written by that well-known
and highly respected firm of " Me, Somebodyelse & Co."   As
it is, I can, if not proudly, at least very truthfully, assert
that—" alone I did it ;" and I am, furthermore, fully justi-
fied in asserting that not one word is TRANSLATED FROM
THE FRENCH.

It is perhaps due to myself, to observe that each and every
portion of the Scrap Book grew out of some " strong and

present impress of the mind." For instance, the Additional Verse to the National Anthem was written when, as is the nation's custom, England's bright sword was drawn, and the scabbard laid aside, on the declaration of war with Russia.

" Up with the Standard of England" about the same time.

" The Battle of the Alma" on receipt of the news of that glorious passage of arms.

The song of " Florence Nightingale" was written when, as now, a whole world loved her for her gentle deeds.

The songs of the " Blue Jackets," " Jack Anchor," " The British Volunteers," &c., &c., about the same exciting period

" I'd rather be an Englishman," was written, with a hope fully realized that a free and happy nation would gladly endorse the sentiments it contained.

The Poem of " Little Jim " grew out of a melancholy bereavement in the mining districts, which came under my own immediate notice.

It is, I presume, quite unnecessary to state when or why I wrote the Royal Marriage Song, seeing that an entire population are as yet scarcely recovered from a national hoarseness, consequent upon the loyal and vociferous shoutings on the great occasion that gave rise to it.

I cannot permit the present opportunity to pass without thanking, which I most sincerely do, all those who have with great kindness, permitted the introduction into my Scrap Book, words of songs, the Copyright of which I had sold to the respective parties.

This, I think, is all — in fact, perhaps more than I need have said to my immediate friends, or an ever kind and indulgent public. And now for the Critics. What shall I say to them : or, rather, what will they say to me? "Aye, there's the rub." Humbly, then, and with most deferential respect, O, most learned Thebans, I crave your mercy. Take not, I beseech ye, "a kitchen poker to kill a mouse." Treat me, I conjure ye, with the contempt I merit. Don't deign to notice me at all—it will serve me right ; and I, oh glorious escape, shall creep out easy. But if, *in terrorum*, it is essential that I should be immolated on the shrine of your well-engendered ire, then let me ask, as a special favour, that you "lay on heavy and dispatch me quick."

> " You bear a mighty scourge, I pray you spare it,
> But should ye not, why I must grin and bear it."

Then bethink ye, dread beings, how far nobler it would be, passing by all such pigmies as myself, if you were to set lance in rest against some worthier mark ; or, in common parlance, just to hit one of your own size. Do this, and O, gentle Sirs, deign to leave alone one who has the honour to subscribe himself,

Your own and the Public's

Very respectful, obedient, and humble servant,

EDWARD FARMER.

Derby, August, 1863.

CONTENTS

Royal Marriage Song.

WRITTEN ON THE OCCASION OF THE ESPOUSALS OF ALBERT EDWARD, PRINCE OF WALES, WITH THE PRINCESS ALEXANDRA, OF DENMARK.

HAIL! Albert Edward, Prince of Wales, a glorious title's
   thine,
Thou brightest star of England's hope. and Brunswick's
   mighty line :
A Nation happy 'neath the rule of thy dear Mother, prays
That God may bless and prosper thee throughout thy future
   days.
Daughter of Denmark, Royal Maid, without one doubt er
   fear,
Take thy proud place among us—we bid thee WELCOME
   here !
All pomp and pageant shall attend, due homage shall be
   paid,
Old England gladly ratifies the choice our Prince hath made.

And now ring out the merry peal, bid brazen trumpets
   sound,
Let cannons roar, from shore to shore, while mirth and
   joy abound ;

Reign, bliss triumphant, rich and poor, both old and young
    be gay ;

Thus celebrating, as we ought, our Prince's Wedding-Day.

See, proudly waving, England's flag, on steeple, dome, and
    tower,

Unsullied lends its graceful folds, to deck the nuptial hour.

Music sends forth its dulcet tones, while oft doth Echo ring,

As from the crowd, bursts high and loud, "God bless our
    future King !!!"

Oh, these are pleasant sights to see, and grateful sounds to
    hear,

While prayers are heard, whose every word, is *heartfelt* and
    sincere.

If love and loyalty may serve to turn all ills aside,

A sunny path awaits thee, Prince, and thy young lovely
    Bride !

And now again with music's strains, with dance, and jocund
    song,

Bestrew with flowers, the passing hours, and happiness
    prolong ;

While hearts are bounding merrily, and eyes are beaming
    bright,

Let all be gay, and make this day replete with fond delight.

While joy-lights shine, fill sparkling wine, and drink with
    love and pride,

Health ! and God's blessings on "The QUEEN !" "The
    BRIDEGROOM !!" and "The BRIDE !!!"

"Little Jim," or the Collier's Home.

"MAN MAY EDUCATE THE HEAD, NATURE ALONE CAN TEACH THE HEART."

THE cottage was a thatched one, the outside old and
    mean,
Yet everything within that cot was wondrous neat and
    clean ;
The night was dark and stormy, the wind was howling
    wild,
A patient mother sat beside the death-bed of her child —
A little worn-out creature, whose once bright eyes were
    dim —
It was a collier's only child, they called him " Little
    Jim."
And, oh! to see the briny tears fast hurrying down her
    cheek,
As she offered up a prayer, in thought, she was afraid
    to speak,
Lest she might waken one she loved far dearer than her life,
For she had all a mother's heart, had that poor collier's
    wife.
With hands uplifted, see she kneels beside the sufferer's
    bed,
And prays that *He* will spare her child and take herself
    instead ;
She gets her answer from the boy, soft fall the words
    from him —
" Mother, the angels do so smile and beckon little Jim.

I have no pain, dear mother, now, but oh! I am so
        dry,
Just moisten poor Jim's lips once more, and mother
        don't you cry."
With gentle trembling haste she holds a tea-cup to his
        lips,
He smiles to thank her, then he takes three little tiny
        sips ;
" Tell father, when he comes from work, I said 'Good
        Night' to him ;
And, mother, now I'll go to sleep." Alas! poor little
        Jim.
She sees that he is dying, that the child she loves so dear
Has uttered the last words that she may ever hope to
        hear.
The cottage door is opened, the collier's step is heard,
The father and the mother meet, yet neither speak a
        word ;
He feels that all is over, he knows his child is dead,
He takes the candle in his hand and walks towards the
        bed ;
His quivering lip gives token of the grief he'd fain
        conceal,
And, see! the mother joins him, the stricken couple kneel,
With hearts " bowed down with sorrow," they humbly ask
        of Him,
In Heaven once more to meet again their own poor
        " LITTLE JIM."

The Gipsy's Prophecy.

A young Maiden met with a Gipsy one day,
    And crossing her palm with a coin,
Said—"Dame, you tell fortunes—at least, so they say —
    And I wish very much to know mine."
"So you shall," said the Gipsy, and taking her hand,
    Looked stedfastly on it awhile :
"You will shortly be tied, dear, in Hymen's silk band "
    "But, to whom ?" asked the Maid, with a smile.

"To one," said the Gipsy. "whose hair is dark brown :
    His eyes ! yes, his eyes are light blue."
"What nonsense !" the Maid said, affecting to frown ;
    But she thought, "Well, if this should come true !"
"He is tall, and good-looking," continued the Dame,
    (The Maiden looked monstrous prim !)
"And I could, but I will not, reveal his dear name "—
    Said the Maid, "She must surely mean —him."

The Maiden was happy, and so was the crone,
    As twinkling her merry dark eye,
She mutter'd, "How vexed she'd have been had she known
    That the man of her heart was close by !"
So it was—for the Swain that the Sybil foretold
    Should marry this Maiden so true,
Had hid where alone the old jade could behold ;
    And so her prediction came true !

The Death of the Miser.

WITH clammy hands and lab'ring breath,
His dim eyes glazed by coming death;
Shivering with cold, mere skin and bone,
In a dark room, and all alone,
Without one friend or comfort nigh,
An aged Miser lay to die.
With groan protracted, long and deep,
He wakes from out a troubled sleep;
And o'er his pale and sickly face
A ghastly smile hath left its trace;
Faint, brief, and transient in its stay,
Like sunshine on a winter's day.
Again, the old man smiles, and see!
All shrunk and wither'd tho' he be,
His wasted form with pain he drags
From 'mong a paltry heap of rags,
On which for years he'd laid his care-worn head.
The wealthy Miser had no other bed.
With weak and trembling step he steals
Across the floor, and lo! he kneels;
But not in prayer—no, 'neath that board
Where he hath knelt, his gold is stored;
And, as with last expiring strength,
He lifts the secret door at length,
And feels (for 'tis too dark to see)
His treasured coins, his ecstasy
Exceeds all bounds, as thus he whispers low,
" 'Tis here! 'tis mine! but not a soul must know!"

Hark ! hark ! he 's counting, one, two, three :
Oh ! that a human mind so sunk should be—
The ruling passion truly to the last —
As one by one, the worshipped coins are passed
Through his lean fingers, how their chink
Deep in his sordid soul doth sink.
That so employed a man should be
On the threshold of eternity !
Is there no better feeling that may part
This fatal passion from the old man's heart ?
Alas ! there is not—gold and gold alone
Can warm a Miser's heart, to all besides 'tis stone !
Still, still, he 's counting, still the old man kneels,
Till o'ertaxed, brain alike and reason reels,
Dispelled by sudden madness, darkness flies,
The Miser sees, but with a madman's eyes.
And now to him his gold appears
Bedewed with weeping orphans' tears ;
And pass before him, one by one,
Good deeds that he MIGHT have done ;
While actions, which he deemed unknown,
Are to his aching vision shown ;
And blood, aye blood ! all red and gory,
Help to fill the mind's mad story ;
For if 'twere true, as rumour told,
In far off lands, the Miser sold
His fellow man, *whose only sin,*
Was being born with darker skin !
He closed his eyes, 'twas all in vain,
There was the slave, the whip, the chain ;

While frantic mothers, pointing wild
To fatherless and starving child,
In accents of deep hate inquire,
For how much dross he sold its sire?
" Take, take, he cried, in tones of wild affright,
These fearful visions from my tortured sight,
I will restore"—! when the stern tones of fate,
Hissed in his ears, the fatal words, Too Late!
With one wild shriek, one loud unearthly yell,
Never again to rise, the wretched Miser fell;
Trembling with illness, howling with dismay,
The spirit of the Miser passed away.
Could not his almost boundless wealth
Purchase one single hour of health?
No! the fell tyrant claims his own,
For all the gold that e'er was known.
Bankrupt in body, as in mind,
He died, and left his gold BEHIND!

Hurrah for the Brave.

In a just cause once more, from old Albion's shore,
    Are departing her valiant sons,
As heard from afar are the wild notes of war,
    And the boom of the foemen's guns.

Oh, they weigh not the cost of the blood 'will be lost,
    Or the dangers they have to go through,
But they go in their might, for their country to fight,
    And the proud haughty foe to subdue!

CHORUS.

    Then hurrah for the brave, on the land or the wave,
        Who beneath England's flag shall be seen,
      And may God grant him power in the battle's dread
        hour,
        Who fights in the name of our Queen!

Shall it ever be said that our country is dead
    To the call of her sons in distress?
Or would idly stand by, while for help they should cry?
    Where, where is the man would say, "Yes!"
In our dear native land, from its scabbard each brand
    Would leap of itself, were it known
That old England refused, when her sons were ill-used,
    To protect and take care of her own!

CHORUS.

    Then hurrah for the brave, &c.

— - - - - —

Song of the Soldier's Wife.

No; I ne'er could have loved him so well as I do,
Though to me he was ever kind-hearted and true,
Had he listened at all to my womanish fears,
Or neglected his duty through my selfish tears.

I remember, with feelings of pleasure and pride,
How gently, yet firmly, my wish was denied;
Saying, " Dearest, I love you — you know that I do —
And all, save my honour, I'd forfeit for you ;
But now, when my regiment is thus called away,
You would not — you could not — desire me to stay."

" No, dearest," I answered, " I feel that you're right,
With a woman's best blessing go forth to the fight,
And join as you should the brave spirits that go,
To curb the pretensions of Albion's proud foe.
On, on, to the conquest, and should I repine,
I deserve not to have an affection like thine."
" Adieu !" cried the soldier — the war trumpet's blare,
With the tramp of the war-steed, rang loud thro' the air,
He's away to the battle, and lost to her view —
He, loyal and tender ; she, faithful and true.

The Best Picture.

In search of a Matsys' why wander —
     After Claude, Cuyp, and Rembrandt why roam —
Our time and our money why squander,
     When we've far better Pictures at Home ?
For alike when the joy-lights are gleaming
     In palace, gay castle, or hall,
Or the cotter's bright ingle is gleaming,
     'Tis the " Shadow of Friends on the Wall !"

Oh! believe me, I would not speak lightly
 Of one soul-gifted, glorious name,
Which serves to illumine so brightly
 The undying volume of Fame.
Still, still, when both Claude and Teniers
 Indistinct on the memory fall,
We shall fondly look back through the vista of years
 To the "Shadow of Friends on the Wall!"

The Last Word.

A GREY-HEADED couple were sitting
 One night in their chimney nook,
The old dame was engaged with her knitting,
 Whilst he bowed his head o'er a book.
The kettle, a "steam tune" was singing,
 The cat purred a song to herself,
And the fire its bright glimmer was flinging
 O'er the old pewter plates on the shelf.

Said he, "Here's a sentence worth heeding,
 'Tis what makes life sunshine or cloud,"
And then the old man began reading
 The following passage aloud :
"'Tis not when dark trouble is round us,
 Or Misery's entered our door,
Or the deepest misfortune hath found us,
 That the temper is apt to boil o'er.

"But it is in the absence of sadness,
    When there's nought to occasion our tears,
When our hearts should be bounding with gladness,
    That this demon of discord appears.
Oh! beware the first word that is spoken
    At all to unkindness akin ;
For I've known hearts grow cold, aye, and broken,
    Through what in mere jest might begin.

"I've known houses made wretched and lonely,
    Do you ask how all this has occurred ?
From this simple cause, and this only,
    The trying to have THE LAST WORD!"
Said the old dame, "'Tis sadly too true,
    'Tis the parent of trouble and pain ;
And I'll tell you, love, what you shall do,
    Turn that leaf down, we'll read it again."

Impromptu.

WRITTEN IN ONE OF THE ALCOVES AT OLD VAUXHALL, BIRMINGHAM,
MARCH 6, 1850.

EACH passing day doth filch away
    Some joy for which it stands our debtor,
And on we range, from change to change,
    Not always, mark ye, for the better.

The time draws near – another year
   Shall see the work of centuries fall ;
For 'tis decreed—sad news indeed,
   To do away with Old Vauxhall !

There's scarce a heart that will not start,
   No matter what its rank or station,
And heave a sigh when they destroy
   This favourite place of recreation.
If we look back on Memory's track,
   What joyous scenes we can recall,
Of happy hours in its gay bowers,
   And friends we met in Old Vauxhall.

There, fine old trees, the passing breeze
   Hath kiss'd for many a long, long year;
This season gone, are every one
   Doomed to come down, and disappear !
Beneath their shade fond vows were made,
   As e'er "Virginia" heard from " Paul,"
For Cupid held an annual court
   For years and years in Old Vauxhall.

Enough, enough, 'tis maudlin stuff,
   I think I hear my readers say,
Houses are better far than trees,
   And Old Vauxhall has had its day.
The pride and pleasure of the town
   It long hath been, it now must fall ;
Improvement wills it, so prepare
   To bid adieu to Old Vauxhall.

Then let the fête, the dance, the song,
  Be gayer now than e'er before ;
Let young and aged swell the throng,
  To view what soon shall be no more.
Let its last season be the best ;
  One blaze of triumph at its fall ;
Let farewell visits be the test
  Of what we feel for Old Vauxhall !

— —

"A few Fishing Lines, or a Challenge to Anglers."

As the following highly pretentious effusion was written some years ago,
solely to oblige, and at the earnest instigation of my much-esteemed
friend, Matthew Tertius Skull, Esq., I am bound to put myself right
with the lovers of the angle, and others their admirers, by clearly stating,
that I by no means endorse the exalted opinion he appears to enter-
tain of his own abilities, beyond the fact of quite going with him, as
regards the acknowledged excellence of the artificial baits he alludes
to, and that of "REDDITCH" being "THE MART" for hooks, &c., of
all descriptions (*wholesale* of course) ; for my own part, I know little of
fishing, beyond what grows out of a very ardent love of the pursuit.

I've read with very perfect pleasure
" Ephemera's Waifs," each line a treasure ;
Have oft perused old "Isaac"* too,
With maxims quaint—yet wondrous true ;
From other authors, good and bad,
All kind of theories I've had.

---

* Walton.

One genius hath writ a book, on
The proper way to tie a hook on!
Another gives a huge discourse
On hair, as had from cow or horse,
And points the difference; then he says,
Worms may be scoured in various ways,
And maggots bred (now this is clever)
From putrid meat—"well, did you ever!"
As if the butchers did not know,
Who daily see the blue-fly blow.
A learned Theban, writes a volume,
In which he doth devote a column
To telling how (good worthy soul)
A man "had ought" to bait a hole;
And to elucidate takes pains,
The mystery of grubs and grains;
And then with "master-mind" doth treat
The abstruse subject of stewed wheat
As an appliance. After which
He mentions, and I hold it rich,
"That grubs of wasps are easiest found
When wasps are making nests around."
It ain't just arrant botheration,
But smacks of super-arrogation!
Poor P, whose style is somewhat odd,
Writes a huge work upon the "Rod."
Sure one who knows so much about one,
Had never ought to be without one.
I've learned to manufacture flies
Of every mortal form and size.

I do not mean that I can make them
As Blacker * does—but fishes take them.
I've just enough of what's termed "nouse,"
To build an artificial "mouse"
Or "frog," to nature's model true—
"The Archimedean minnow" too,
Quite equal to the " Derby-killer," †
For which men part with so much siller;
Although the maker, sooth to say,
Has killed some rattlers in his day;
Mine take the lead, none e'er denies,
Of those so noted by Allies. ‡
I've made an imitation new worm,
Between a "brandling" and a "dew-worm,"
And recommend my friends to try 'em,
No fish with fins on, will go by 'em.
Spoon-baits (congenial) are my pride,
All competition is defied.
For Gimp, and Gut, and Hooks I'm derry
To all those kind of things, Sir, very;
And if a man's a mind to shackle,
And purchase his own fishing-tackle,
Bid him his wayward course to steer,
To famed REDDITCH, in Worcestershire;
There he can purchase fitting hooks,
From ocean fishing down to brooks.

---

* A famous maker of artificial flies.
† Mr. Warren's destructive bait, of Derby, is here alluded to.
‡ A very killing bait manufactured by him at Worcester.

I'll bottom fish, or troll for pike,
Or whip a trout stream, which they like ;
I'll spin a minnow, dib with drake,
For fifty pounds aside, and stake
With any piscatorial elf,
Who's game enough to back himself.
Some amateurs presume to speak
Of mighty deeds performed at LEEK.*
I fear them not, alike I take
From river, pond, from pool, or lake,
The scaly tribe ; and as for roach,
I've caught enough to load a coach ;
With paste and gentles, malt that's stewed,
How I have thinned that "red-finned" brood!
Aye, and how justly proud I feel
Of the mode in which I bait for eel.
The Barbel mystery I'll unravel,
Who poke their leather snouts in gravel.
With bullocks' pith, their favourite grub,
I've killed some hundred-weights of "Chub."
For "Carp" and "Tench," when weather's clear,
Wind in the south, and "wheat in ear,"
Of surface weeds just mow a bit out,
And I'll be bound to clear a pit out.
In fact, I'll meet the challenge gaily,
Of any man excepting "BAILY ;" †
Letters addressed, Post Office, Hull,
Will find me always — — M. T. SKULL.

* An extensive and beautiful sheet of water, more than two acres in
width, in Staffordshire.
† The Champion Fisherman of Nottingham.

My Garden.

'Tis many, many years ago, when I was quite a child,
And at a time, too, I've been told, when I was sadly spoiled,
My mother, bless her sainted form (for she is dead and gone),
Was speaking of a garden, and I said, " May I have one ?"
" Yes, my own darling," she replied, "you shall, and very
     soon ;"
And we picked the spot, a darling plot, that very afternoon.
Not proudest florist, though he culls bright flowers from
     zone to zone,
Could ever rival in effect, that garden of my own.

I think I see it now, as plain as ever it was seen,
The border made of oyster-shells, and little walks between ;
The mustard and the cress I grew, the radishes so fine,
And lettuces (I don't believe there e'er was such as mine).
The daisies wild and primroses, I'd gathered in the lanes,
And violets' bloom, whose sweet perfume, right well repaid
     my pains.
My father, bless him ! planted me a rose tree, and it grew ;
I'd snowdrops, and I'd crocuses, white, yellow, striped, and
     blue.

Ah ! those were happy times indeed, for all around was gay,
But father, mother, garden, all, alas ! have passed away.
Since then I've witnessed many scenes of misery and joy ;
But I've not forgot my garden yet—in fact, I do not try.

Fond memory clings to simple things, when greater are
     forgot ;
And oft in fancy I return, to that dear happy spot—
Where 'neath a mother's gentle care (now mouldering in her
     grave),
I spent the happiest hours I've known, in the garden that
     she gave.

The Blind Boy.

From murky clouds, fast hurtling round,
Bursts the loud thunder's deafening sound ;
Quick follows each electric flash,
Roar after roar, crash after crash !
While torrent-like the rain doth pour.
" Who comes in such a fearful hour ?
'Tis poor old Martha's withered form
Thus braves the fury of the storm,
With hurried and unequal tread ;
Uncovered, too, that aged head.
What can have happen'd ! What 's amiss
To bring her through a storm like this !
Run, Harry, to the door, and see
What the poor creature's troubles be !"
Thus said the father to the son.
The boy with willing haste hath run,

And ope'd the door to one whose face
Bore sorrow's past and present trace.
" Why, Martha," thus began the boy,
" Why look so pale ? — What makes you cry ?"
"Oh ! Master Henry—oh !" she said,
" My child, my poor blind child is dead !
Struck, struck by lightning !"   Then on the floor
She shuddering fell, to rise no more !
Of friends, of fortune, long bereft,
With only that one heartstay left —
That son to whom she 'd given birth
Was all that bound her soul to earth :
For him she 'd labour'd long, had borne
This world's privations and its scorn !
For those who know her history tell
She "loved not wisely but too well."
That sightless pledge, her only joy,
Her poor, her blind, neglected boy !
Now all was ended — this sad blow
Fill'd to the brim her cup of woe.
Enough of life was left to tell
The death of him she lov'd so well :
This latest, saddest grief express'd,
Her broken spirit sank to rest.

The Deep Blue Ocean.

Oh! I love the deep blue ocean,
　With its bright and glistening spray,
Where the rolling tide's glad motion
　Speeds the dancing foam away ;
And the bold wind wh'stles gaily,
　As it plays among the shrouds,
And the sea, one glorious mirror,
　Reflects the passing clouds.
　　　　Oh! I never feel so happy,
　　　　　So joyous or so free,
　　　　As I do upon the ocean,
　　　　　So the deep blue waves for me !

And when the tempest gathers
　Its mighty force around,
And dark clouds, charged with thunder,
　Burst forth with deafening sound —
E'en then my buoyant spirits
　Mount high amid its roar,
Nor would I change its dangers
　For the pleasures of the shore.
　　　　Oh! I never feel so happy,
　　　　　So joyous or so free,
　　　　As I do upon the ocean,
　　　　　So the deep blue waves for me !

Old Monarch.

THERE was ice on the river, and snow on the ground,
    The wind whistled bitterly cold,
When a worn-out, half-famished, and footsore old hound
    Crept cautiously into the fold.
The shepherd perceived him, as coiled up he lay,
    And rated poor Monarch right well,
Who rose uncomplaining and went on his way,
    Where to, and what for, I shall tell.

Time was when old Monarch, a fine leading hound,
    Was petted by rich and by poor,
Not then, I presume, could a shepherd be found
    To turn the brave hound from his door.
Howe'er, let that pass, as all things must do,
    Poor Monarch no longer was young,
No longer was first subtle Charley to view,
    No longer the first to give tongue.

Just heed the poor fellow, as onward he goes,
    Nor hunger nor cold does he mind,
With the blood oozing out from between his poor toes,
    The grave of the huntsman to find.
With love unabated, and instinct all true,
    He crawls, where at last he is found,
To the grave of his master, 'twas all he could do,
    But it proved him a faithful old hound.

The Standard of the Free.

Music may be had of Messrs. D'Almaine, London.

Hurrah for the Standard that's waving!
  Fondly clasped in the arms of the sea,
Each danger and obstacle braving,
  O'er this home of the brave and the free.
Beneath its blest shadow the fetter
  Of slavery ne'er can be known ;
Oh, tell not of lands that are better,
  There's none like this land of our own ♭
     Hurrah for the Standard that's waving,
       Fondly clasped in the arms of the sea,
     Each danger and obstacle braving !
       O'er this home of the brave and the free.

The cloud that has lately hung o'er it,
  Prosperity's sunshine shall clear,
Chasing want and misfortune before it,
  And wealth and content shall appear.
The foul voice of treason hath frighted
  Fair Commerce away for awhile ;
Yet fear not, for all shall be righted,
  And Commerce return with a smile.
     Hurrah for the standard that's waving,
       Fondly clasped in the arms of the sea,
     Each danger and obstacle braving
       O'er this land of the dauntless and free.

Go, ask the Untaught Savage.

Go, ask the tattoo'd Indian where
 The God HE worships deigns to live —
Go, ask the untaught savage, where —
 And mark the answer he shall give!
He'll tell you that there's not a place,
 Above, below, or all around,
But if ye, sorrowing, seek His face,
 The God of Mercy may be found!
There's not a planet in the sky
 But lighteth where "the Spirit" lives;
There's not a zephyr murmurs by
 But whispers of the peace He gives;
There's nothing in the heavens or earth,
 The mighty ocean or the air,
Or aught from either has its birth,
 But His Omnipotence declare!
Then, Christian, kneel, bow low thy head,
 And think on what the savage said.

A FLATTERER'S tongue is oiled by bad intention, and set in motion by deceit.

Is it Love?

[Published by the permission of Mr. W. T. Belcher, Birmingham, to whom the copyright belongs, and where the Music may be had.]

HEY! sing hey, and hi sing oh! what's the reason Kate's
    so low?

Powers above now, is it love now? 'pon my word, I'd like
    to know!

Once her merry laugh went ringing, making music through
    the house ;

Now she's gloomy, sad and moping, and as silent as a
    mouse.

Short time since, a smile was ever on those pouting lips
    of her's,

But now in nooks, with downcast looks, she pensive sits,
    and seldom stirs.

Hey down derry ! ho down derry ! what's the reason Kate's
    so merry ?

Powers above now, is it love now? it looks uncommon like
    it – ver-y !

Here's a clatter !—what's the matter?—why this rushing
    up and down '

Halloa, you, sir! what's to do, sir? "Captain B's come
    back from town !"

Look at Kate now! -hear her prate now, bless her little
    noisy tongue !

Gay as ever, sighing never, thinks all dulness very wrong?

Beam and rafter ring with laughter, eyes are glist'ning as
    before ;
Beyond all doubt the secret's out, for Katey is herself
    once more.

Hey down derry ! ho down derry ! what's the reason Kate's
    so merry ?
Powers above now, is it love now ? it looks uncommon like
    it—ver-y !

The Subscription Pack.

[The Conclusion of the Season, with an account of certain matters
connected therewith.]

THE season is over ! no more shall we hear
The music of hounds, or the huntsman's glad cheer ;
No longer on wings of the breeze shall be borne
The crack of the whip or a sound of the horn.
Sly Reynard may now take his foraging prowl
In search of a rabbit, a duck, or a fowl ;
Or, prompted by love, he may wander about,
Without the least danger of being stopped out.
The kennels, how altered ! the flesh-pot is cold ;
The oatmeal, though clean, is by no means so old
As that on which daily the pack had been mess'd ;
It is finer, yet cheaper, and has not been press'd ;
When made into paste (but perhaps I may wrong it),
I fancied I saw some *"mashed taters"* among it.

Coats, caps, whips and spurs, are put carefully by,
The saddles are covered, and hung in the dry ;
And, fearful that stirrups and bits should get spoiled,
They are first nicely cleaned, and then properly oiled.
There's a draft from the stud, all the lame and the old,
With a few (just as "ticers") are sent to be sold ;
The rest in "loose boxes" o'er fetlocks in clay,
Are fed upon oats (that are "kibbled") and hay.
As the weather gets warmer I haven't a doubt
They'll be most of them "blistered" or "fired," and turned
    out !
There's a strong smell of whitewash around and about,
They are clearing the ticks and the cobwebs all out.
The committee are here, it's surprising to see,
Now the hunting is over, how "stingy" they be.
All is turned into money, the bones and the dung ;
The hounds have been "weeded," some sold and some
    hung ;
And the "Management" know what each item is booked at—
Economy now, is the only thing looked at.
They've been holding to-day, what the blacks call "a talk"
As to where they shall send out some puppies to walk.
And letters are written, beginning with "Dear
Mister (blank), we have sent you a Fox-hound to rear,
Who is told by the whip 'tis a favour to get him,
And is begg'd not to feed him too fat nor to pet him ;
That the bitch (to the grief of the hunt) is a dead un',
That his sire is first class and a capital bred un'.
So the huntsman felt anxious to have the pup near him,
Nor could think of a person so likely to rear him !

He was out of old "Bountiful," gotten by "Chorister,"
Quiet at nights, and they'd christened him "Forester;"
And by way of just gently watering his back,
Said the last one he reared is the pride of the pack.
And I feel pretty certain and greatly afraid,
There is nowhere such "tricks upon travellers" played,
As with us! and the reader may think we abuse 'em—
But it's seldom indeed that the Farmers refuse 'em;
And then it is only with "hairy-heeled coves,"
For around us are living "good woolled uns" by droves,
Who have no hesitation in standing their pound
Towards kennel expenses and keeping a hound.
To such, and preservers of foxes, long life,
A home blessed with plenty, a good temper'd wife,
A nag that can carry him twice in a week,
For I love a good fellow, and hate every sneak.
When I make you aware that I once lived at Meynell's,
You won't be "supprised" I know something of kennels.
I am glad I have written, for I quite set my heart on it,
Though I'm bound to admit our first whip* did a part on it·

If it were as difficult to make a promise as a "pig-trough,"
what an awful diminution of the article in question would
accrue! It might even have a deleterious effect upon the
law courts—Eh?

---

* PAUL PUGSLEY, now Huntsman to the celebrated "Catch 'em-who-can'
Pack of Foxhounds.

In Humble Reliance.

WHEN the cold hand of Death shall be laid on this heart,
　　And this now throbbing pulse shall be still,
When the soul, tired of clay, shall with rapture depart,
　　To wherever my Maker shall will.

Great God, in Thy mercy and wondrous power,
　　Sustain and support my last breath,
And grant to my spirit, in that fearful hour,
　　A trustful submission to death.

Strong, strong in the faith of Thy holy blood spilt
　　Upon Calvary's Mount for our sins,
Teach, teach me, O Lord (for Thou canst if Thou wilt),
　　That 'tis only in Death Life begins.

To the mansions of bliss bid my soul take its flight,
　　Through Thy blood be my sins all forgiven,
And with angels all beautiful, holy, and bright,
　　Let me rest with my Saviour in heaven,
　　Bid me rest with my Saviour in heaven.

——— ———

CONSCIENCE is not proud—is not above speaking to persons,
let their circumstances be what they may.

The Fair Maid of Trentham.

WRITTEN ON THE MARRIAGE OF LADY EVELYN GOWER WITH LORD
BLANTYRE.

Let the cannon's loud roar to the bells' tuneful peal
Tell forth, in glad chorus, the joy that we feel ;
Let echo, with notes of delight, swell the choir,
For the " Fair Maid of Trentham " is " Lady Blantyre."

See ! Scotia's famed land of the mountain and wave,
At the shrine of our fairest hath yielded her brave :
Far blest above others be ever that hour
When the blood of the Stewart was blent with the Gower.

All hail to thee, Trentham ! beneath whose proud dome
Meek Pity and Charity both find a home ;
Where Cupid hath lit Hymen's holiest fire,
Forging fetters of love for the Lord of Blantyre.

Daughter of Sutherland, bright be thy brow,
By sorrow unclouded, and sunny as now,
Thy grief never greater than 'tis at this hour :
God bless thee ! thou beautiful child of the Gower.

Come, fill up the wine cup, fill, fill to the brim—
On its surface let prayers for their happiness swim !
May heaven's protection and best gifts conspire
To bless the young Lord and the Lady Blantyre.

The Jackdaw and the Starling.

[Written expressly for a little boy to learn and sing. Aye! and he did
learn and sing it too - famously! as may any other little boy, or " child
of riper growth," if he so will it.]

THERE was once a little Starling
   Lived in a hollow tree,
As pretty a little Starling
   As you'd ever hope to see.
He had everything he wished for ;
   For sitting by his side,
Was another little Starling,
   And that Starling was his bride.

He had lots of wool and horsehair
   To build his summer's nest,
And you'd think if ever Starling was,
   That Starling would be blest.
But Envy was the Starling's bane,
   (As 'tis of many people—)
And all because two old Jackdaws
   Were building in a steeple !

" Over my head," the Starling said,
   " They fly with outstretched wings,
Nor notice me, in this poor tree,
   The proud, conceited things !

Oh, how I hate my lowly fate !"
  These were his foolish words ;
Nor are these envious feelings all
  Monopolized by birds.

One day the wind was blowing hard,
  He sat with upturned eyes,
When out the Jackdaw's nest was blown,
  And through the air it flies.
All the poor throng of unfledged young
  Were dashed upon the ground ;
And then, and not till then, the truth
  Of this "old saw" he found—
Which tells alike of men and birds,
  Of great as well as small,
The higher up we build our nests,
  The further we 've to fall !

Empromptu.

[Written on the subject of that never-to-be-forgotten fearful Accident, at Hartley Colliery, January, 1862, by which horrid catastrophe Two Hundred and Seven Persons were hurried into Eternity.]

Hark! a loud cry of anguish rends the air,
And none are silent, save where mute despair
Hath choked all utterance—where, with pallid cheek,
A wife or mother vainly tries to speak!
Fathers, in agony, look trembling on,
Whose son or sons down that dread shaft have gone;
And all is misery, grief, and dark dismay
At Hartley Colliery on that mournful day.
Not all are paralysed, strong men are there,
Who, spite of danger and the dread foul air,
Work on in willingness by night and day,
Doing in earnest all that mortals may
To drag from the jaws of Death their comrades—brave
If any yet might live in that gigantic grave,
Masters and men alike, with noble, feeling hearts,
In that "sad drama" bravely played their parts.
Oh, but 'twas terrible, that dire suspense!
Freezing the blood, benumbing every sense,
Till, from the yawning abyss, men appear,
Whose looks are ghostly, fraught with livid fear,
And from their pale parch'd lips (some shrieking fled)
Fell the appalling sentence—ALL ARE DEAD!
There are no words that may express that scene,
'Twere well in pity, perhaps, to draw a screen

O'er frenzied feelings, and the mad despair
That all, or nearly all, that stricken district share.
God, in Thy mercy hear our humble prayer,
Teach these bereft ones their great loss to bear—
Learn them to bow 'neath Thy Almighty will ;
Be to the fatherless, a Father still—
Soothe in her hour of woe, the widow's heart—
Snatch from her bosom, Pain's relentless dart:
Give peace, O Lord, to every tortured breast—
Help Thou the weak, and succour the distress'd.
And now for England : What will England say,
Or rather do, to keep despair away ?
Who, that knows England, has a moment's dread
That these lone sufferers shall have daily bread,
And all such help as their sad case demands ?
England has tender hearts, and helpful, willing hands ;
And as, on startled ears, the direful tidings fall,
One common feeling will pervade them all.
On to the rescue ! England to the fore !
And " Hartley Colliery " rings from shore to shore !
Our Queen ! God bless her, 'mid her own vast grief,
Shall listen to her heart, and send relief,
One glorious rivalry : 'tween rich and poor,
Shall drive stern want from every sufferer's door.

———————

As prussic acid acts upon the body so doth pride upon
the soul.　Avoid both.

King Steam.

HURRAH for the rail ! for the stout iron rail,
  A boon to both country and town,
From the very first day that the permanent-way,
  And the far-famed fish-joint were laid down.
'Tis destined, you 'll find, to befriend all mankind,
  To strew blessings all over the world.
Man's science, they say, gave it birth one fine day,
  And the flag of King Steam was unfurled.
    Then hurrah for King Steam, whose wild whistle and
        scream.
    Gives notice to friends and to foes,
    As he makes the dust fly, and goes thundering by,
    So stand clear and make room for King Steam.

Aye ! a monarch, I say, hath he been from the day
  He was born ; on that glad happy hour,
Until now, when we know the vast debt that we owe
  To his daring, his speed, and his power !
See the birds left behind, as he outstrips the wind,
  By the aid of key, sleeper and metal.
Great Watt little thought what a giant he 'd caught,
  When the infant was boiling a kettle.
    Then hurrah for King Steam, &c.

They may tell, if they will, that our monarch can kill,
  'Tis a fact, I admit, and well known,
But fairly inquire, and there 's this to admire,
  The fault is but RARELY his own.

With the high and the low, he 's his failings we know,
  And his moments of weakness, no doubt.
Since the world first begun there were specks on the sun,
  Then why should King Steam be without ?
    Then hurrah for King Steam, &c.

Old Morgan the Miller.

A JUDGMENT.

OLD Morgan got up, and old Morgan sat down,
And he got up again in a flurry,
Struck the dog, kicked the cat, then laid hold of his hat,
And left home in a deuce of a hurry.
Whate'er can it be that has vexed the old man,
And so put him about as all this ?
The secret I 'll tell, he saw Rob, at the well,
Give his niece, gentle Mabel, a kiss !
Well, well, you inquire, is that just cause for ire ?
For young folks will be young folks still :
It perhaps may be so, but old Morgan, you know,
Won't have such goings on at the mill.

Old Morgan has hastened across the long mead,
Old Morgan has turned up the lane,
Old Morgan is looking so angry, indeed,
As he ne'er would look pleasant again.

He has reached the farm-house of his neighbour Rob Dean,
He has shouted his name at the door,
And has asked young Rob's father what such doings mean,
Such work as he ne'er saw before.
" Hold ! hold !" cried his neighbour, " come in and sit down
Such matters are easy to cure ;
Come give us a smile, and get rid of that frown,
For it all will come right I 'm quite sure.

" I 've something to tell you, I know you 'll be glad —"
" If 'twill please me," said Morgan, " why, speak !"
" Then, sweet Mabel, thy niece, and my good-looking lad,
Have been married for more than a week."
" The deuce !" shouted Morgan, " if that be the case,
Though they 've acted both foolish and wrong,
Yet the matter shall rest, for I once did my best
To do ditto when I was as young.
But the maiden was stupid, or else it was I,
For she went and she married my brother,
And the maiden with whom I once acted so sly
('Tis a judgment !) was Mabel's own mother."

The Marchioness of Lorn.

WRITTEN ON THE MARRIAGE OF THE LADY ELIZABETH GOWER
WITH THE MARQUIS OF LORN, JULY 31, 1844.

AGAIN glad marriage bells are ringing!
Sounds of joy each breeze is bringing:
Banished hence be grief and care;
The Gower hath wed with Campbell's heir!
True loving hearts and noble hands
Are joined in holy wedlock's bands.
Again, from Trentham's Ducal Tree,
Scotland, a branch we give to thee!

Son of the mighty Campbell's race,
Thou 'rt welcome in thy pride of place;
In proof of which, is given thee,
In all its native purity,
A PRICELESS PEARL! A COSTLY GEM!
Would grace a royal diadem!
A heart where only virtues live —
This, Marquis, is the Gem we give!

And now uprouse the joyous strain,
Let only mirth and pleasure reign.
Raise high your goblets fill'd with wine;
The Thistle and the Rose entwine:
May their bright path be strewn with flowers,
Their life one round of blissful hours:
May Heaven's blessing e'er betide
" The Campbell " and his lovely Bride.

I'd Rather be an Englishman.

[Set to music, and may be had at Mr. J. Shepherd's, Newgate Street,
London.]

I 'd rather be an Englishman,
    Whatever may betide,
And boast the proud possession
    Of an Englishman's fireside—
I 'd rather have old England,
    As the land that gave me birth,
With all the faults they charge her with,
    Than any place on earth.

The rabid voice of anarchy
    May rave 'bout other climes,
But have they more of freedom there ?
    Or have they better times ?
Is liberty of kinder growth—
    Oppression quite unknown—
Or are the blessings they enjoy
    Superior to our own ?

The answer's No ! a thousand times repeated—No ! and then
A world's wide echo takes it up, and thunders No ! again ;
May no vile, frantic love of change, destroy or set aside
Those fine old Institutions for which our fathers died.
Sedition is, and ever was, a nation's greatest curse,
And only has the tendency of making bad things worse ;
Convinced of this, come, let us join in one true loyal band,
And die for (if we 're called upon) our Queen and Native Land.

    I 'd rather be an Englishman, &c.

Florence Nightingale.

[Music may be had of Messrs. D'Almaine, London.]

A PRAYER for Florence Nightingale, and the goodly little
    band
Of tender hearts, who, mercy-bound, have left their native
    land,
To nurse our suffering heroes, who have nobly fought and
    bled —
To soothe them in their hour of pain, and tend the sick
    man's bed.
Oh, woman! gentle woman! thy high mission is to bless,
Alike when we are happy, or when sunk in deep distress,
This act of self-devotion should make, and so it will,
Woman, to every manly heart, more dear and cherish'd still.

It needs no stimulus, we know, to make our brave men fight ;
It is enough they are at war for Freedom, Truth, and Right ;
But yet methinks, 'twill nerve each arm, and make each
    heart beat high,
To think, if they are wounded, there are English nurses
    nigh !
Then, bless thee ! Florence Nightingale—thou true and
    gentle maid,
And all who in pure loyalty shall lend to thee their aid.
And when no longer shall be heard the angry cannon's roar,
We'll welcome thee, with grateful hearts, to England's
    happy shore.

Have Faith, and Fear not.

BEHOLD the sunset !—gorgeous sight—
O'er land and sea a flood of light,
　　Like burnished gold.
To other lands he wends his way,
'Tis eve to us, to them young day
　　His gates unfold.

Say, who can view, without delight,
Yon glorious, grand, and solemn sight ?
　　The sun departs !
So when deep grief a scar hath made,
And sin and error cast a shade
　　On human hearts.

When lives are darkened by regret,
Our sun of happiness is set,
　　Yet hope lives still.
And banish'd sorrow, grief, and pain,
The sun of joy may rise again,
　　If 'tis His will.

Then bid defiance to Despair,
To dark Despondence, canker'd Care,
　　And all their crew.
Be sure that He who gives us light,
Who rules the sun, with all its might,
Would ne'er condemn to endless night
　　Myself or you.

Nuptial Song.

WRITTEN ON THE OCCASION OF THE MARRIAGE OF LORD
GROSVENOR WITH THE LADY CONSTANCE GOWER.

DUNROBIN the Pibroch is sounding on high,
Which Lilleshall echoes with fervour and joy ;
Whilst Erin, famed Isle of warm hearts, tunes the strings
Of Leinster's sweet harp, and wild melody flings
To England's gay shore, where, with joyful acclaim,
Are mingled the Granville and Grosvenor's name ;
Argyle's loyal clan meets without cross of fire,
And pleasure rings loud in the halls of Blantyre.

See, nobles assembled in bridal array,
For the fair Lady Constance is married to-day !
And there at the altar, just objects of pride
To the parents of each, are the bridegroom and bride ;
And many a fervent and soul-whispered prayer
Is wafted to Heaven to bless the young pair—
For by all who are present 'tis easily seen,
'Tis but giving the hand where the heart long hath been.

On, on to the banquet, bid Sorrow take flight,
This day is devoted to purest delight !
Not a trouble or grief, or a sigh must there be,
From Sutherland House, Noble Eaton,* to thee ;
Not a tear but is mirth-born must glisten to-day,
But pleasure triumphant make each bosom gay.

---

* The seat of the Marquis of Westminster.

Who would mar with one care the delights of this hour,
Is not true to the Grosvenor or friend of the Gower.

Now raise every goblet filled high with choice wine,
The honour of giving the toast shall be mine :
" The Glorious Chain of Nobility " drink,
To which Grosvenor and Granville this day add a link !

Mark Mansfield or the Two Ricks of Hay.

A MODERN PASTORAL.

MARK MANSFIELD, the mower, was merry and blythe,
   As the lark that sung over his head,
And he joked with his mates as he whetted his scythe,
   And gaily he laughed as he said,
" I remember this leasow when I was a lad,
   And the young master here quite a child :
There was such a swath, and the mowing was bad,
   And it druv' my poor feyther half wild :
For himself and Joe Griffis had taken the job,
   At so much per acre, to do —
And to find their own drink — so you'll easily think
   'Twas a deuce of a job for them two!

"And the old master came on his pony and smiled,
  And unto the mowyers did say,
'Stick to it like bricks, it 'll make two good ricks —
  When it 's made, lads — of capital hay.'
Then my feyther spoke up, and said, 'Master, I know
  You 're a very good master, indeed ;
In fact, both myself and my Butty here say,
  You 'm the best master ever we seed !
We don't mean to shirk it, but, master, look here,
  We 've worked like two Niggers all day,
So, master, God bless you, just stand us some beer,
  And you shall have two ricks of good hay.'

"Then the master he gi'd the old pony a kick,
  And he said, as he canter'd along,
'I 'll stand you a gallon for each of the ricks !'
  And he did, and he sent it 'um strong !
My heart, how they leather'd away at their job,
  My feyther, poor mon, and old Joey,
And at night when the master came round on his cob,
  They 'd both got as drunk, lads, as Cloey.
I well recollect, I 'd to help my dad whum,
  And Griffis's wife h.ped her master,
'Twas the talk of the village and every one said,
  That no bottles or scythes e'er went faster !"

CONSCIENCE is the soul's "safety-valve"—that attended
to, all is well !

Prepare.

AGAIN in the distance the war-dogs are growling,
    Dense clouds black as Erebus darken the air!
The vulture's wild scream to the wolf's dismal howling,
    'Mid cry of the Eagles bids Europe — PREPARE!
Dear England! thy duty lies plainly before thee;
    'Tis due to thy children, as faithful as free —
'Tis due to the Queen, who so mildly reigns o'er thee,
    To prepare for whatever the fates may decree.

Yet having prepared, may no sense of false honour
    Induce thee to join in a cause not thine own;
But if any should dare to fix insult upon her,
    England's mode of returning an insult is known!
No longer she heeds whatsoe'er it may cost her
    (All feelings save honour at once set aside) —
What true son of her's, if that feeling were lost her,
    Would look on her longer with love or with pride?

Collected and calm, as becomes a great nation,
    Await the events that thou may'st not control;
In attitude peaceful maintain thy proud station,
    While happily by thee the war-tide may roll;
But if, in defence of thy soil or thy freedom,
    Rude war is forced on thee in spite of thy care,
Whoever thy foes, dearest England, ne'er heed 'em,
    Thou hast but one duty, it is — To PREPARE!

Too Short for the Service.

I 'LL sing you a song of a cobbler,
    Who lived in the Town of Tralee ;
His name it was Anthony Dobbler,
    And a very smart fellow was he.
He worked at his stall all so gaily,
    He whistled and sung like a bird,
Till, poor fellow, he saw Judy Bailey,
    Which altered the case, on my word.

       O dear ! O dear!
    When Cupid once gets in the way,
    Be it Dustman or Duke, Lord, Coachman or Cook,
    The urchin they 're bound to obey.

For now he sits glumpish and moody,
    Never a whistle or song ;
Can it be all Mistress Judy ?
    Or what upon earth can be wrong ?
O some folks will say that he waited
    On Judy to ask might he woo ?
When sad on his ears these words grated,
    " No, Anthony, that will not do."

       O dear ! O dear ! &c.

" For I love a lad who is fighting
    In foreign lands, far, far away,
Who the wrongs of his country is righting,
    So don't you stay longer, I pray."

"I'll speak to your father," says Dobbler,
　"I'll speak to your mother, likewise ;
Be a soldier instead of a cobbler,
　If they do not object to my size."
　　O dear ! O dear ! &c.

Then he hastened away to the " Lion,"
　Where the drum and the fife he heard played,
His fate and his fortune to try on,
　For he meant to make warfare his trade.
The shilling he got in a minute,
　And the standard they reached, when, O my !
It was clear there could nothing be in it,
　He was just four feet ten inches high !
　　O dear ! O dear ! &c.

"Too short," says the sergeant, " by gorry !"
　" I'll put on my shoes," says the snob :
"That won't do," says the sergeant, " I'm sorry,
　But you're rather too short for the job."
Says Dobbler (however unwilling),
　" I must give up all thoughts of the wench ;"
So the sergeant and he spent the shilling,
　And the cobbler still works at his bench.
　　O dear ! O dear ! &c.

SELF-LOVE is commendable ! if the person possessing it be above reproach — not else.

The Lunatic's Foresight.

ONE morning in May, a fair maiden so gay,
  Came tripping it over the moor,
And if truth, sirs, I tell, this same charming young belle,
  Had been there several mornings before.
The heather was blooming—that MIGHT be the cause,
  Wild strawberries were ripe to the hand,
Whilst the views round about were right lovely, no doubt,
  And THEY might induce her to pause,
  And THEY might induce her to pause.

Yet she stoops not to gather the sweet blooming heather,
  Nor strawberries, ripe though they be,
Nor for beautiful sight turns to left or to right,
  Till she reaches the old hawthorn tree.
And, see in the distance, a youth wends his way
  To that very identical spot !
Now, it really seems strange that two persons should range
  So soon on the moor—does it not ?
  So soon on the moor—does it not ?

The murder is out, there'll be anger and ire
  (Mark my words) very soon in that quarter,
When the Squire comes to know that the keeper's son, Joe,
  Is presumptuously courting his daughter.
O Love ! but for thee this fair maiden would be
  In bed, I've no doubt, and a sleeper ;
But by Love driven mad, see the foresight she had,
  To provide herself thus with a keeper !
  To provide herself thus with a keeper !

An Appeal to the Rats—by One of Themselves.

"On Tuesday night, at Shaw's, Bunhill Row, his little dog, Tiney, weighing only 5½ lbs. killed two hundred rats in fifty-six minutes and fifty seconds." Vide *Bell's Life*.

[Kindly inserted in *Bell's Life*.]

Ye rats of England — if there still remains
That love of idleness, of dirt, and drains,
Which your bold ancestors from Norway brought,
When years ago this sea-girt isle they sought —
Brown, black, or white, large, middle-sized, or small,
I charge ye, listen to a patriot's call !
No matter where your residence may be,
If by the water-side or hollow tree,
Ye lie contented in some moss-lined nook,
And calmly listen to the murmuring brook ;
Whether in lordly pile or cottage bred,
In well-stored barn or under pigstye bed ;
If bean rick hold you, or you fix your seat
In barley staddle, or in thatch of wheat,
Behind a wainscoat, or beneath a floor,
I ask your presence, and I ask no more.
Be ye but ready, and ne'er heed how rough,
Though bred and nurtured in " a common sough,"
Wrongs ye have suffered, wrongs, too, tamely borne —
The time is come ! discard the yoke you 've worn !
Shall all things else with liberty be blessed,
And rats alone have evils unredressed ?

Forbid it, injuries too long sustained !
Forbid it, rights long lost to be regained !
Come from your holes, concentrate all your powers,
And justice, liberty, and revenge are ours.
Shall that fell despot, man, with tyrant power,
Heap wrong on wrong, increasing every hour
The huge indignities, and we submit ?
No ! rather let Sedition's fire be lit,
And all the consequences of internal strife—
The loss of blood, of credit, and of life.
And the reaction which we know succeeds.
When the best interests of a country bleeds.
Regardless of all this, divine and human laws,
Up rats and arm ! get ready teeth and claws ;
Be this our war-cry, " Down with men and buffers !"
'Tis all for freedom ! so ne'er heed who suffers !
'Tis not enough that ferrets, Hob and Jill,
Are taught to hunt us out, and dogs to kill
In honest warfare, but by traps we're caught,
And (hear it all of ye) in bags are brought,
Huddled together—nay, suspend your rage—
And foully murdered in a cockpit cage.
Go, search the columns of last Sunday's *Bell's,* —
And note the horrid butchery it tells.
One Shaw, of Bunhill-row, hath got a tyke
(Sure mortal ears ne'er listened to the like),
Who did—oh, sickening and appalling sight—
Destroy two hundred rats on Tuesday night !
And dogs did yelp, and men did shout and laugh,
While this small canine, *five pounds and a half,*

Trained by his owner this vile deed to do,

Made many a widowed rat and orphan too.

Further I shall not say, except with tooth and claw,

Pitch into all your foes, especially old Shaw;

And do it rats at once, for you must see, of course,

The little good that's got by merely moral force.

One brief short sentence more—Be bold! and *verbum sat*,

A small subscription* raise for yours,

An Old Buck Rat.

* There that's exactly what I expected; the old rat winds up just like all the rest of these would be patriots, with a hint about giving him summat. It's a nation strange thing they never can, somehow, get their feelings to rise higher than their breeches pockets. They're all alike for that. Printer's Devil.

'Tis Wonderful what we can Do if we Try.

[Published by the permission of W. T. Belcher, Esq., Birmingham, to whom the copyright belongs, and where the Music may be had.]

I'm fond of old maxims, they serve to convey,

A vast deal of truth in a very brief way;

For instance, take this one, which none can deny,

It's wonderful what we can do if we try!

What a beacon of hope in this sentence we find!

What a spur to exertion it lends to the mind!

Neglected full half of our energies lie;

Oh, it's wonderful what we can do if we try!

Whatever our station in life, but look round,
Some object of pity is easily found,
The aged, distress'd, or the young let astray,
Are by no means uncommon, I 'm sorry to say.

To banish cold Want from the sufferer's door ;
O'er the spirit that 's wounded, soft pity to pour
The tears of the widow and orphan to dry ;
Oh, it 's wonderful what we can do if we try !

How sad to imagine the fault may be ours,
That many are weeds that were meant to be flowers ;
There are plenty (God, help them !) now guilty and bad,
Had been better if different teaching they 'd had.

And where, in this strange, busy world, would I ask,
Is so glorious a labour, so grateful a task,
As to cheer up the hearts of the wretched with joy ?
And it 's wonderful what we can do if we try !

By a Victim.

[Kindly inserted in *B ll's L fe*.]

Mine, Mr. Editor, is no theme to jest on,
For I've been humbugged, middled, got the best on,
Dropped in the hole, sir, flummoxed, done, and cheated
In fact, I've been "picked up," and vilely treated.
Sir, you must know, myself and Philip Frazer --
A pal of mine, a plumber and a glazier
(I feel that from the bag the cat I'm letting).
Are now (and always have been) fond of betting .
I do not mean we go and put the *pot* on ;
But when a "sov" or "fiver" can be got on,
We're game to risk it, and the fault's not ours,
If hunting after sweets we nap some sours.
The picking out a horse to win, you mark,
Is something like snipe shooting in the dark :
The very shot and powder, mind, would blue it,
A man must shoot so long before he'd do it ;
But preaching's all my eye - there's nothing in it.
We know that there's a flat born every minute,
And they are wisely sent sir, never doubt 'em,
For what a figure sharps would cut with at 'em !
But to my story : Philip, t'other night,
Met (as it proved) a "wide-awake" young wight---
One of those noisy chaps with sun burnt faces
And capacious breeches, that you see at races.
Now Philip having crossed his hand with gold,
Was by the little downy villain told

That he was willing, and, moreover, able,
To tell the secrets of each trainer's stable ;
He said, for instance, Bowe's Springy Jack
Was nothing better than a common hack ;
That Surplice was a " book horse," nothing more,
And said, in fact, that he had heard him roar ;
" You bet against him," were the words he said,
" And don't be frightened, he's as good as dead !"
I've not a moment's doubt he was a " bonnet,"
But be that as it may, we acted on it,
And I conceive a perfect right we've got
To be for evermore among GREEN's lot !"

I. NOET,

Late of Droppet Hall,
Now of Skinner Street, London.

The Blue Jackets.

[Set to Music, and may be had of D'Almaine, London, to whom the
copyright belongs.]

WHAT! a Sailor hang back when there's war on his tack !
Why, what blessed moonshine good laws !
Let the foe fire a gun, Jack would fight him for fun,
　　Let alone our most glorious cause,
　　Let alone our most glorious cause.

Then what folly to prate (as some folks have of late),
 'Bout this Czar and his millions of men,
 'Mid the battle's loud roar we have conquer'd before,
And we're able to do it again jolly hearts,
And we're able to do it again.

What matters to him, where his vessel may swim,
This has been and will be his plan,
With his friend, the Marine, Jack will fight for his Queen,
Nor ask 'bout the size of his man.
He blesses his eyes when he hears with surprise,
That all hope of Peace is not gone :
Yet sees such wild work between Russian and Turk,
And longs in his heart to make one, jolly hearts,
Jack longs in his heart to make one.

Jack will ne'er disobey, but he will have his say,
And he mutters, Why all this 'ere fuss ?
We can safely depend upon France as a friend,
Then why not just leave it to us ?
Every man is prepar'd, let but War be declar'd,
And the Banner of Battle unfurl'd,
Bar colour, nor size, ourselves and Allies,
Are fully a match for the world, jolly hearts,
We are fully a match for the world.

Song.

[WRITTEN ON THE OCCASION OF THE MARRIAGE OF THE LADY CAROLINE LEVESON GOWER WITH THE MARQUIS OF KILDARE.]

Gay banners hang upon the wall,
And pleasure reigns through Trentham Hall;
While every breeze that floats around
Comes laden with some joyous sound;
In dulcet notes distinct and clear,
The Harp of Erin's tones we hear;
And lords there are, and ladies fair
To greet the Marquis of Kildare.

And see! fond blushing by his side,
Is Lady Caroline—the Bride!
For they to "Holy Church" have gone,
And spoken words have made them one.
Full many a fervent heartfelt prayer
Was uttered for that noble pair,
That Heaven with choicest gifts would bless,
And grant them health and happiness.

Great Chief of Sutherland! we view with pride
Thy noble branches spreading wide;
Long may the "Star of Trentham" shine,
And blessings wait on thee and thine!
Now fill with sparkling wine each glass,
While gaily round the toast shall pass,
Drink with sincerity as I propose—
The Shamrock and the English Rose!

'Tis Lovely May.

[Published by the kind permission of W. T. Belcher, Esq., Birman ham to whom the copyright belongs, and may be had of D'Almaine & Co., London.]

'Tis lovely May, all nature's gay,
    The violet blue is flinging
Its sweets around, and joyful sound
    The notes of wild birds singing.
The primrose pale perfumes the gale,
    The hawthorn lends assistance,
While through the dells the village bells
    Are ringing in the distance.
While through the dells, the village bells
    Are ringing in the distance.
Then dance and play, drive Care away,
    Nor let its shade come o'er us.
Our path's not clear, yet never fear,
    There's sunshine on before us.
    There's sunshine on before us.

Shall birds and flowers have happy hours,
    And man alone be sad,
As if kind Nature had not lent
    Enough to make him glad ?
There's not a creature born on earth,
    From greatest to the small,
But what has cause for thankfulness,
    And man above them all

Then dance and play, drive care away,
    Nor let its shade come o'er us,
Our path 's not clear, yet never fear,
    There 's sunshine on before us.
    There 's sunshine on before us.

Cheer up! and keep on Never Minding.

[Published by the permission of W. T. Belcher, Esq., Birmingham, to
whom the copyright belongs, and where the Music may be had.]

LET sages rave, with visage grave,
    To prove this world's beyond all bearing,
But ne'er forget, some warm hearts yet
    Are left, which make it worth the wearing.
If clouds should lour and friends look sour,
    'Tis only neighbours' fare you're finding ;
One maxim still cures every ill —
    Cheer up! and keep on never minding.

One thing's quite clear,—no mortal here
    Hath happiness without some sorrow ;
And though to-day, joy flies away,
    It may come back again to-morrow.
No hour so drear, but in its rear
    Some warmer, brighter tint is winding ;
Then come what may, play out the play—
    Cheer up! and keep on never minding.

David Dobson.

A TRUE TALE.

DAVID DOBSON and his missis
  Lived a very happy life,
Had their share of worldly blisses,
  Little knew of worldly strife.
Wealth they 'd none, nor did they need it,
  Health they had, an l so were blest.
If great folks frowned, they did not heed it,
  Envy never marred their rest.

They 'd a little house, and garden
  Which David till'd with his own hand :
David did not care a " farden "
  For the richest in the land.
They 'd a little cow and dairy,
  They 'd a little pig and sty,
They 'd a daughter like a fairy,
  With auburn hair and mild blue eye.

Proud was David of his daughter,
  Prouder still was his good bride,
Till, sad to tell, Consumption caught her,
  And their gentle Bessie died !
Mark ye, how the picture 's alter'd,
  In the garden, weeds grow wild,
If neighbours noticed, David falter'd,
  It 's no use now, I 've lost my child '

A Capital Run with the United Pack.

[Kindly inserted in *Bell's Life*.]

Mr. EDITOR: Sir,— As your columns abound
With all sorts of sports, from the racehorse and hound
To a show of canaries, permit me a space
To describe an unusual, but excellent chase,
That came off near our village a few days ago,
And was well worth the seeing, as quickly I'll show.
A pig (Nay, don't start, Sir!)—a grunter, I say,
Who had got (as pigs oft have) a very bad way
Of "rooting" (that's proper, as every child knows)
The bricks from the floor of his "sty" with his nose ;
So offended his owner by conduct like this,
That he sent for the blacksmith to shove through the gris-
Tle (or cartilage rather, for that's the just phrase),
A ring that should teach this vile pig better ways.
The morning and Vulcan are duly arrived,
And he who in similar ingoes had strived
With porkers before, got the waggoner's lad
To lay hold of his tail, and the notion warn't bad !
'Tis by no means essential, I fancy, to tell
How the lad got upset, or the noseborer fell,
'Tis enough that it was so ; the pig, a real boar,
Made a put at the closed, but yet ill fastened door,
And away, like blue blazes, the varmint was seen,
Going straight as a dart over Faddlemore Green.

To rise and to whistle, and holloa like mad
For the sheepdog and Pincher, and order the lad
To run and get round him—quite proper to do:
But the swine had got four legs, the lad had but two—
Was the work of a moment, every dog in the place,
Men, women, and children, all join in the race:
There was plenty of racket, as you may expect,
But the pace was severe, and the "field" got select—
The "Snieder" has cut it, the "Cobbler," his friend,
With Miss Marklew's fat footman, have "bellows to mend."
First Flightmen alone had a chance it was clear,
And they had to play all they knew to keep near.
This prince of all pigmeat full two miles had gone,
Yet still full of running, his course he held on:
The pig, through the open, sends on like the wind,
Leaving "Welters" and "Craners" and slow uns" behind.
Hold hard! there's a check! but not long did it last,
He's viewed in the orchard, the fatal die's cast—
A mastiff of Haydon's had chanced to be loose,
Which rendered his dodging and game of no use;
He pursues and o'ertakes him, and into a ditch,
Knocked him head over heels, when a broken-haired bitch
Of Ratcatcher Roden's led on the gay pack,
With murderous intent, on the poor porker's track;
Oh, had you but heard how they made the place ring,
As though "Hullah" had tutored each canine to sing,
Till they came to the worry, when sad to relate,
They "settled his hash" ag'inst Latimer's gate
Myself and two others, Joe Briggs and his friend,
Were all that unluckily witnessed the end;

But his owner arriving, just at the last push,
Gave me the pig's bristles to make me a brush.
Say why should our nobles abroad ever roam
In search of wild boars when we've such pigs at home ?

Kate of Norton Vale.

[Published by the kind permission of Mr. B. Williams, London, to whom
the copyright belongs, and where the Music may be had.]

THE birds were singing sweetly,
   Wild flowers were blooming gay,
When I lost my heart completely
   In the merry month of May.
'Twas morn when thirsty Nature
   Was busy drinking dew,
When fair in form and feature,
   Dear Kate first met my view.
Her steps had fairy lightness,
   Her hair was raven dark,
And from her eyes of brightness,
   Shone forth the soul-lit spark.
From this cold world thou 'rt vanished,
   Yet memory's self must fail,
Ere thy lov'd form be banished,
   Sweet Kate of Norton Vale.
   Sweet Kate, Sweet Kate of Norton Vale.

Thrice cruel Death to sever
    Two hearts by love made one;
Though Kate, thou 'rt gone for ever,
    I still love fondly on.
But, oh! 'tis useless grieving,
    My only joy shall be
The bright hope of believing
    That I may come to thee.
From this cold world thou 'rt vanished,
    Yet memory's self must fail,
Ere thy dear form be banished.
    Sweet Kate of Norton Vale.
    Sweet Kate, Sweet Kate of Norton Vale.

The Promise.

[Published by the permission of W. T. Belcher, Esq., Birmingham, to whom the copyright belongs, and where the Music may be had.]

How well I remember, when I was a child,
The smile of my mother, so gentle and mild,
As I knelt at her feet in an evening to pray,
In words that dear mother had taught me to say
Again I behold her, with soul beaming eyes,
As with finger uplifted she points to the skies,
Saying, When we have passed through this sad world of pain,
It is there, dearest Edith, I 'll meet thee again,
    'Tis there, dearest Edith, I 'll meet thee again.

Years, years have flown by, since her spirit departed,
  To realms where such spirits are destined to go,
For the good and the faithful, the kind and true hearted,
  Can ne'er be intended for torment and woe.
How often through life, when dark clouds have hung o'er me
  Those words have brought comfort, and banish'd all pain,
And hope, blessed hope held this promise before me—
  'Tis there, dearest Edith, I'll meet thee again.
  'Tis there, dearest Edith, I'll meet thee again.

The Scorpion.

[Printed by the kind permission of Robert Paget, Esq., the owner of the
copyright.]

  ONCE more, once more we're away from the shore,
    On the ocean's wild waters to roam,
  And gay as a bride doth the Scorpion ride,
    As she scuds through the dancing foam.
  With a captain and crew, as daring and true
    As e'er were afloat on the sea,
  The saucy old jade is pursuing a trade
    Only fit for the dauntless and free.

  And now on the chase we are gaining apace,
    Quick! on toward our victim we go;
  Down, down from its height comes the streamer white,
    And the blood-red flag we show!

See ! see ! on her shrouds all her canvas she crowds,
 The Trader perceives his mistake,
From the red flag he knows that the worst of all foes—
 The old Scorpion — lies in his wake.

In vain do they fly, they must strike or must die,
 No mercy from us will they find ;
As well may they think the huge ocean to drink,
 As to leave the gay rover behind.
We near her ! the shout of the battle breaks out !
 We board ! all her gold is our own !
'Neath the fathomless wave they have met with a grave,
 The old Scorpion is sailing alone.

Impromptu.

TOO GOOD TO COME OFF.

IN a half-timber'd cottage, in some quiet nook,
 With some fifty good acres of land,
With a spinney for rabbits, some trout in a brook,
 A small garden and orchard at hand,
A snug kitchen corner for cold winter nights,
 A glass of good ale for a friend,
One dear smiling face to put all things to rights,
 Would to goodness kind Fortune would send.

Grant these, and a fig for the town and its joys,
    Its constant excitement and riot !
Far more country places and customs I prize ;
    Give me their pursuits and their quiet !
Go ! Luxury, far from my humble abode ;
    Content ! deign to enter my door ;
Pride ! take back thy soul-killing heart-breaking load,
    I am free ! and I 'll bear it no more !

Sweet Peace ! with thy presence enlighten my cot ;
    Blessed Health ! make my chamber thy home,
Mild Happiness ! come and complete my proud lot,
    Then never again will I roam.
Unruffled and calm will I thus end my days,
    Till my head is laid under the sod,
My parting hour gilded by Hope's gentle rays,
    In the goodness and mercy of God !

Flowers and Weeds.

[Inserted by the kind permission of J. B. Williams, Esq., Paternoster Row, London, to whom the copyright belongs.]

THERE is no lack of bliss in a bright world like this,
  Though midst the sweet flowers that abound,
A weed here and there in our path should appear,
  A stray nettle or thistle be found.
There is no joy on earth but by contrast has birth,
  Then why should we grieve or be sad,
By kind Nature 'tis shown that both must be grown,
  Just to show us the good from the bad.
      Then come let us be gay, and sing while we may,
        And prove to the world by our deeds,
      Though small merit be ours, when taken as flowers,
        We are no kin at all to the weeds.

Nature also makes known, by the seeds she has sown,
  The blossoms she'd wish us to bear,
Nor desires that one bloom be o'ershadowed with gloom,
  Or canker'd by sorrow and care.
And so if you find a poor flowret, the wind
  Of misfortune hath broken and toss'd,
Oh, haste to restore to sunshine once more!
  A flower that is otherwise lost.
      Then gay as before—yea, a thousand times more,
        For happiness grows on good deed! —
      Go, join the glad throng in the dance and the song
        And leave all the cant to the weed!

Come, Come, Merry Hearts.

Come, come, merry hearts, nor play sadly your parts,
  In the drama of Life we 've assigned us,
Let us sing and be gay, as the wild birds in May,
  Leaving Care, the old varlet, behind us.
Let the goblet and bowl chase all grief from the soul,
  Be good humour the guest of to-night,
While in bumpers we toast the dear girl we love most,
  And by singing put Sorrow to flight.
    For the grape was designed for the good of mankind,
      And the juice of its berry we know,
    By Dame Nature was sent with the kindest intent,
      To lessen the world of its woe!

Then be not ungrateful, refuse not to taste
  This antidote sent to our pain,
Bright hours like the present were not sent us to waste,
  Once gone boys, they 'll ne'er come again.
Old Time in his might as he urges their flight,
  When he sees us so merry and blythe,
In his trembling hand, though he carries the sand,
  May forget the sad use of his scythe.
    For the grape was designed, &c.

Never judge by outward appearances. Who would ever imagine there was milk in a cocoa nut?

The Rifleman's Song.

[Published by the kind permission of Joseph Williams, Esq., 123, Cheap-side, London, to whom the copyright belongs, and from whom the music may be had.]

RECIT.

Hark! hark! hark! 'tis the sound of the bugle!
List! list! list! 'tis the beat of the drum,
As with hearts light and gay as the wild birds in May,
The Volunteer Riflemen come!

SONG.

John Bull, he looks glum, for wild rumours are come,
Which engender suspicion and doubt;
John prepares for the storm, and bids Riflemen form,
And all true sons of his to turn out,
And all true sons of his to turn out;
And he hums to himself, as he jingles his pelf,
"Invasion, the thought I can't bear it;
But if they come here, there's one thing quite clear:
They must win it before they can wear it."

CHORUS.

For Johnny's as bold and as true as of old,
There's Paddy with weapon so handy;
Brave Taffy will fight, either morn, noon or night,
And I always can reckon on Sandy.

John Bull, we all know, is remarkably slow
    Ere he pulls off his coat, or he fights ;
But when once he begins, mind he dies or he wins,
    In defence of his Queen and his rights.
Then hurrah ! for the band, who with rifle in hand
    Are prepared to keep foemen at bay ;
And God only knows who are England's foes,
    So hurrah ! for the green and the grey.

How glorious to see, thus united and free,
    The sons of old England prepare,
Who for sweethearts and wives would hold cheaply their
        lives,
    Nor their blood nor their treasure would spare,
    Nor their blood nor their treasure would spare.

Should the war cannon roar on our dear native shore
    (Tho' they'd hail the occasion with sorrow),
There is not a soul in that brave muster-roll
    But would die for old England to-morrow ;
There is not a soul in that brave muster-roll
    But would die for old England to-morrow.

How frequently a man in furnishing his heart and his
house, selects both his wife and furniture less for use than
ornament ; the auctioneer can settle the one, while death
alone (or worse) puts an end to the other ill-advised arrange-
ment.

The Manor House.

[Written expressly for E. P. Addison, Esq. Music by H. W. Du Lang, and may be had at T. Harrison's Music Warehouse, Birmingham.]

THE Manor House was standing here a many years ago,
When from its gate in martial state, they marched to meet
    the foe.
With banners flaunting gaily, and retainers true and bold ;
In those rude times a man must fight for what he meant to
    hold ;
And later still, when civil wars were raging through the land,
" The Chief" of this Old Manor House led forth a loyal band ;
While from its earliest date till now, I've one proud thing
    to say,
That none who ever asked relief went unrelieved away.

And as it was, so shall it be, for firm our motto stands,
Which we have borne for centuries—"Warm hearts and
    ready hands."
For, oh ! how sad a thing it is that we should e'er refuse
A trifle to the needy, when we've more than we can use.
Good deeds beget true happiness : be merry, then, and blythe ;
There's nothing like a cheerful heart to blunt Time's fatal
    scythe ;
And when at last we come to die, against our faults 't will weigh,
That none who ever asked relief went unrelieved away.

The Old Laburnum Tree.

[Published by the permission of Thomas Harrison, Esq., of 30, Colmore Row, Birmingham, to whom the copyright belongs, and where the Music may be had.]

COME sit thee, dearest, by my side, and listen while I tell
The reason why I love this old Laburnum Tree so well ;
'Twas here in childhood's happy time we used to meet and play,
And memory tells of blissful scenes on many an after day ;
Of't busy fancy conjures up the groups that used to meet
And chat, and wile away the hours upon this very seat :
'Tis wonderful how many things of good and ill there be,
That seem as 'twere to link themselves with this Laburnum
        Tree.

And oft in summer's heat I seek its dear and welcome shade,
And think how like the flowers it bears our brightest hopes
        must fade,
Or when stern winter's chilling blasts have stripped its
        branches bare,
E'en then the tree hath charms for me, it bids me not despair.
For though misfortune (winter-like) some present ills may
        bring,
Bright hours shall follow certain, as Old Winter beckons
        spring,
'Twas planted by a mother's hand, a mother dear to me,
Then can you wonder I should love this old Laburnum Tree.

The Bee and the Butterfly.

[Published by permission of W. S. Belcher, Esq., Birmingham, the owner of the copyright, and from whom the Music may be obtained.]

A BEE and a butterfly, settled one day,
By chance on a rosebud together,
The one was at work, and the other at play,
'Twas morning, and bright sunny weather.
" How do !" said the butterfly, " may I inquire
Why bees all seem destined to labour ?"
" We think of our home, when dark winter shall come,"
Replied his industrious neighbour.

" O fiddle-de-dee, leave off work, come with me,
And spend a gay life mid the flowers,
There is summer and spring," said the gay thoughtless thing,
" To say nothing of autumn's glad hours."
But the bee shook his head, and with honey he fled
To those whom he loved, while his friend
Continued his flight, sipping sweets left and right,
Little thinking how soon it would end.

But a few months gone by, when this proud butterfly
Was met by the bee in distress
His coat not so gay, as when first seen in May,
And his pride and his consequence less.
The sunshine was gone, of bright flowers there were none,
And passed were both autumn and spring,
But unlike the poor bee   no provision had he,
So he died a poor heart broken thing.

Up, up, Dearest Sister.

Up, up, dearest sister, by first dawn of day,
Ere Sol's gentle rays chase the dew-drop away,
Where the grasshopper chirps, and the merry wild bee
Hums a note full of gladness, when birds from each tree
Their matin songs carol to welcome the morn,
And green fields bid welcome to flowret's fresh born,
Where the murmuring brook dances gaily along,
O come, gentle sister, and join the glad throng,
O come, gentle sister, and join the glad throng.

Let those that may chose it make cities their home,
Be it our happy lot through the wild woods to roam,
Where trees in their majesty wave over head,
And the wild thyme and violet make their sweet bed,
While the zephyrs sing music that angels might hear,
And the blue vault of heaven shines brightly and clear,
In suppliant posture, dear sister, we'll fall,
And offer a prayer to the Maker of all,
And offer a prayer to the Maker of all.

———

Never form a friendship with a man that children will not
go to, and dogs will not wag their tails at.   There's more in
it than you'd fancy.

The Retired Tradesman.

"AN OWRE TRUE TALE."—*Burns.*

MR. MORTIMER MAXWELL had given up trade,
For this excellent reason : his fortune was made ;
He hath freehold and leasehold, and copyhold too,
So Maxwell bethinks him of what he shall do ;
   He no longer will stay,
   But at once cut away
   From the vile smoky town,
   To a "Cottage Orneé."

Now Mortimer Maxwell hath found a retreat,
A not over large one, but monstrous neat ;
It hath little green shutters, a little green door ;
But I'm telling too much, I shall mention no more.
   A paper was stuck up,
   On which it was told
   The Cottage would either
   "Be Let," or "Be Sold."

He has taken and furnished the "Crib" very nice ;
He went for the nobby, he heeded not price ;
His chairs, and his tables, and carpets, were new,
His "plate" second hand, but that's nothing to you ;
   While the doings o'er head,
   From the best damask bed
   To the meanest utensil,
   Were good, people said.

There's one thing it grieves me uncommon to say—
To the gloom of his path he'd provided no ray;
As a palpable "Hedge" to a dull country life
He should (so the ladies said) take him a wife;
> And the truth shall be known,
> For the fault was his own,
> That he'd no "flesh of his flesh,"
> Or "bone of his bone."

For mothers were constantly bringing their daughters,
Who "painted on velvet," and "played," from all quarters;
But, with grief be it said, that to happiness dead,
He hinted "at present" he should n't get wed:
> He don't know what to do,
> And the devils so blue
> Come to visit him oft,
> And torment him a few.

At last a near neighbour, a fox hunting squire,
Who Maxwell's "pale brandy" and weed did admire,
Said he'd send him a horse to Spottleback Gorse,
And Maxwell accepted his offer, of course;
> He look'd quite the "cheese,"
> From his "heel" to his "nob."
> As he rode to the "meet"
> On his bonesetting cob.

But it's one thing to meet them, another to go,
As poor Maxwell's exploits in the sequel will show;
They are thrown into "covert," they have found, and are gone;
"Hark! forward! they're running, and Maxwell makes one;

Instead of the rein
He lays hold of the mane,
And he holdeth his breath,
For he's frighten'd to death.

Oh ! why did he mount him, alas ! for the day ;
See, the horse lays his ears down, he's running away :
On ! on ! 'mong the "ruck," over hedge, ditch, and stile,
By dint of the pummel he holds on a mile ;

Till they came to a bullfinch,
When, sad thing to say,
A "purler" went Maxwell,
And there Maxwell lay.

Much bruised was his body, all torn were his clothes,
He has knocked his front teeth out, and flattened his nose,
So that not his best friends would be able to know, sir,
That they saw Mr. Mortimer Maxwell the grocer.

A man named George Smart
Took him home in his cart,
Thus playing a country
Samaritan's part.

Of " hunting " our grocer has had quite enough ;
By the squire he's been christen'd a "Jolly Old Muff;"
Retirement to him has brought nothing but pain,
So he says he shall go into business again.

The Dissembler.

SHE may dissemble, and the world may give
    Her credit for a mastery yet unperformed
O'er feelings that entwine her heart, and live
    By latent love and fond remembrance warmed.

The gaiety assumed to aid disguise,
    By pride engendered, badly plays its part ;
Serves but to herald on a hundred sighs,
    Sad native language of a broken heart.

Is it not maddening that a heart should fall
    A prey to Pride's base mandate, yet
Feel while it bows beneath the baneful thrall
    A love it *would not,* if it *could, forget.*

Jack Anchor.

[Published by the permission of John Shepherd, Esq., 98, Newgate Street,
London, to whom the copyright belongs, and where the Music may
be had.]

JACK ANCHOR was leaving to plough the salt wave,
Not a soul 'mong his messmates more gallant, or brave,
As he stepp'd in the boat as they pull'd from the shore,
To go where guns rattle, and loud cannons roar.

He went with a smile, not a tear dimm'd his eye,
Though his poll and his little ones where standing close by.
"For my Queen," said bold Jack, "I will peril my life,
For I know they'll take care of my children and wife."

Once more to his friends upon shore wav'd his hand,
And departed to fight for his dear native land ;
The vessel he sail'd in has vanish'd from sight,
He is gone in the cause of the injured to fight ;
And 'tis ours, while he's absent in danger's career,
To help and to comfort those Jack holds so dear ;
So from highest to lowest, let each gen'rous heart
In this good work before us take kindly a part.
Then up and be doing, the dark hour is come,
Our warriors are summon'd by trumpet and drum,
And while soldiers and sailors for us risk their lives,
Be it ours to take care of their children and wives.

--- --- --- --

The Angel of Pity.

MEEK Pity descended from bright realms above,
To visit this earth on a mission of love,
In search of a dwelling-place roamed every part,
And at last made her home in an Englishman's heart ;
Nor found the place lonely, sweet Mercy was there,
Hope sat in one corner, and Joy took the chair,
While the smiles that were beaming on Charity's face
Threw a cheerfulness round, and gave light to the place,
Stay, stay, gentle being, nor seek to depart,
From this birthplace of honour — an Englishman's heart.

A widow is weeping in silence and gloom,
The pride of her heart late consigned to the tomb,
Cold Poverty reigns where was Plenty of late,
There's no bread in the cupboard, no fire in the grate ;
The tear-drop is rolling fast down her pale cheek
As she looks on her children so hungry and weak.
The oldest too young to at all comprehend
(God help him !) the loss of his father and friend.
While the youngest of three is a baby asleep,
No wonder despair through her bosom should creep !

Dark thoughts gather round her, her brain is on fire,
As she looks on her offspring, and thinks of their sire,
Lo ! the door softly opens, and Pity appears,
Chases Want far away, and dries gently her tears.
Health ! chief of all blessings, returns to her cot ;
And the widow resigned meekly bows to her lot.
There are deeds in this world to which angels give birth,
Which all may indulge in who live upon earth ;
Aye ! all -- rich and poor, high and low — may take part,
If the angel of Pity but dwells in the heart.

Cheerfulness,

NOT INCONSISTENT WITH GOODNESS—T'OTHER WAY ON! QUITE.

THINK ye God had e'er created
    Flowers that bloom, and birds that sing,
If cheerfulness was what he hated ?
    Don't believe in such a thing.
Think the sun would shine so brightly,
    Azure vault and stars be seen—
Would soft zephyrs dance so lightly,
    Through the meads and forest green ?

Think ye there is sin in gladness,
    That this world was made for grief,
And all mankind condemned to sadness ?
    What has taught you such belief ?
Not the blessings that surround you,
    Not the mercies you have known,
If dread and gloomy fear hath bound you,
    Be sure the fault is all your own.

DOUBTS are the rocks on which our mental vessels split in
the great voyage of inquiry after truth !

Hurrah! for the Red and the Blue!

[Music by Charles Coote, Esq., to whom, conjointly with myself,
the words and music belong.]

THOUGH the fears of some folks I don't share,
   Still it's all very well to prepare,
In order to show, both to friend and to foe,
   That we're able a contest to bear;
   Beyond this, if the foeman should land
   On our dear little free native strand,
There are hearts bold and true, there's the Red and
    the Blue,
   Between England and danger to stand.
      Then hurrah! for the Red and the Blue,
      The gallant, the bold, and the true;
If foemen should come, sound trumpet and drum,
    And rely on the Red and the Blue.

Yet, mingled with Ocean's loud roar,
   Should the "battle-cry" ring on our shore,
In old England's behoof who would dare stand aloof?
   We should fight as we've oft fought before.
   Ev'ry heart that was loyal and true
   Would join with the Red and the Blue;
So if foemen should come, sound trumpet and drum,
   And trust to the Red and the Blue.
      Then hurrah! for the Red and the Blue, &c.

The mild dove of Peace long hath spread
Her soft wings o'er Britannia's head ;
And the blessings we know to her presence we owe ,
Oh ! who would not grieve if she fled ?
But for all that is present and past,
God grant that good feeling may last,
And confusion to he, whomsoe'er he may be,
Who the first stone of warfare shall cast.
Still hurrah ! for the Red and the Blue, &c., &c.

Trot on.

[Published by permission of Messrs. D'Almaine & Co., London, to whom the Copyright belongs, and where the Music may be had.]

On ! waste not in grieving and sorrow
A life that is merely a span,
Nor dream ye too much of to-morrow ;
Making sure of to-day is the plan ;
There's enough in this world to amuse us,
There's plenty of good to be done ;
And if Fortune, the jade, should abuse us,
Let us merrily sing and trot on.
Trot on then, I charge you, and gaily,
Whether heavy or light be your load ,
Trot on, for this truth we learn daily,
That cheerfulness shortens the road
CHORUS — Trot on, trot on, trot on, &c.

Then crying's no cure for our troubles ;
    Long faces do no good at all ;
If the best of our hopes turn out bubbles,
    Laugh, laugh, and they're nothing at all.
'Tis folly to give way to sadness,
    Or in sighs to be wasting our breath,
So if woes interfere with our gladness,
    Trot on boys, and laugh them to death.
        Trot on then, I charge you, and gaily,
            Whether heavy or light be your load ;
        Trot on, for this truth we learn daily,
            That cheerfulness shortens the road.
CHORUS—Trot on, trot on, trot on, &c.

Impromptu

ON THE DEATH OF A MOTHER AND INFANT, THE MOTHER'S
DEATH PRECEDING THAT OF THE CHILD BUT A
VERY SHORT TIME.

YEA, both are departed, the mother and child ;
See, their friends broken-hearted, their anguish is wild ;
Who shall tell but the parent hath stay'd on the road
To guide her loved son to his future abode ?
Hark ! angels with ecstasy welcome the twain,
Who are freed (and for ever) from sorrow and pain.
Then cease your fond grieving, wipe the tear from each eye,
And take comfort, believing their end was pure joy.

The Battle of the Alma.

[Inserted by the kind permission of Messrs. Brewer & Co., Pilgrim gate Street, London, to whom the Copyright belongs, and where the Music may be had.]

THE Russian army gather'd on Alma's rugged height,
Prepared itself for action and dared the coming fight,
Their guns boom loud defiance as from the shore advance,
The red coats of Old England and the valiant sons of France
No bugle's sound or beat of drum fell on the list'ning ear,
But from ten thousand manly throats arose one mighty cheer,
On! on! exclaim'd St. Arnaud; Forward! Lord Raglan cries,
And charging up the rocky steeps, on went the brave Allies.

Oh! the Battle of the Alma
Shall never be forgot,
A blaze on England's scutcheon
On the Russian shield a blot.

All heedless were those warriors of death, or wounds, or pain,
Though bright swords gleam'd like lightning, and shot pour'd
down like rain.
Shoulder to shoulder on they went, doing their deadly work,
Vict'ry or death the only cry of English, French, and Turk;
Until at last on Alma's height as conquerors they stood,
The route they'd ta'en was strew'd with slain, and cover'd
o'er with blood,
Right bravely did those gallant hearts who shared this
glorious fight,
Sustain their country's honour on the Alma's tow'ring height

Oh! the Battle of the Alma, &c.

The Young Slave's Belief.

WHAT you term stars in yonder skies
Are lovelier far — they 're angels' eyes ;
And when looks dim that glorious throng,
They weep that those they love do wrong :
The soft and murmuring winds you hear
Are sighs that precede the coming tear :
My mother's 'mong them ; oft in showers
I 've knelt me down and prayed for hours,
Hoping a tear from her bright eye
Might fall upon her orphan boy.
You 've heard the thunder's awful crash,
And seen the lightning's vivid flash :
'Tis "HIM" in anger, "HE" who gave
Life to the white man and the slave ;
Who will demand the reason why
You thus enslave His Indian boy ;
Will judge us by the heart within,
Nor heed the colour of the skin."

————————

WHO, in the possession of happiness, would be mad enough
to prefer an hour to a day ; a day to a week ; a week to a
month ; or a month to a year? yet is time preferred to
eternity !

Honest Jack.

Being a feeble endeavour to express the well-known keen regret of T. H., Esq., at the loss of a singularly handsome and very good black and tanned terrier dog, which, following his natural love of the same in hunting, unfortunately picked up some poison laid there for the destruction of vermin and so met his death. His kind master did (and caused others to do) all that could be thought of to nullify the dreadful effect of the potent mineral, but without effect; and so Jack died, and was buried under a pear tree in his sorrowing master's garden.

EPITAPH.

Who love not dogs, I bid them to stand free!
A black tanned terrier rests beneath this tree;
Not master's love nor medicine could save
This best of canines from a cold, cold grave;
Sages may cavil at and blame my grief,
Holding that love for dogs is past belief;
And perhaps 'tis not the term one should apply,
But sooth I wept when poor Jack came to die.
And mark, I blush not; cynics may smile on,
Could tears have saved him, Jack had never gone.
My dog was honest, faithful, good, and true;
May I, kind reader, say the same of you?
Well, let that pass, I cannot call thee back;
And so farewell for ever, honest Jack!

Lose the key of the cellar, spoil the lock of the cup,
button up your breeches pocket, give a mouth
to roof, and then count your tri...

The New-born Year.

WRITTEN JAN. 1, 1862.

HAIL! new-born Year, in whose glad face
A thousand promises we trace,
Of worldly blessings, Nature's gifts,
When from the earth the Storm King lifts
His icy hand, and bids appear
Sweet Spring, with visage mild and clear ;
Whose birth the balmy violets tell
To primroses in mead and dell ;
Let every human voice be raised
In one loud anthem—God be praised !

Anon the Summer flowers advance,
As Nature wakes from out her trance ;
Rich Plenty, with an open hand,
Scatters abundance through the land ;
The new mown hay its perfume yields,
And corn in blossom decks the fields ;
Fruits ripe and luscious meet the eye.
Telling of Autumn by-and-bye.
Let every human voice be raised
In one loud anthem—God be praised !

Sun-burnt and laden, Autumn nears,
Tanning with brown the wheaten ears ;
The thankful grain low bows its head
To passing breezes, quickly fled ;

The pimpernel (its hour of pride)
Dares the blue corn-flower by its side,
(While twittering swallows o'er them skim,)
To look as bright and gay as him.
Let every human voice be raised
In one loud anthem—God be praised.

Then comes stern Winter once again,
And follow in his boisterous train
Dense Fogs, and Frost, whose breath doth freeze
The fading leaves on shrubs and trees,
And proffers, as he round doth creep,
To all that need it, rest and sleep :
Until at Nature's beck once more
They rise and flourish as before.
Let every human voice be raised
In one loud anthem—God be praised !

One of those Painful Facts.

WRITTEN AT THE EARNEST REQUEST OF ONE OF THE
"HAS-BEENS."

WHEN I gave dinners and choice old wine,
Plenty of very good friends were mine ;
But when all my dinners and wines were gone
I look'd for my friends, and I had not one!

DAVID DENNIS, Esq

Late of Crab Hall, near Skunnorge

The Morning is Breaking.

HUNTING SONG.

Dedicated to all lovers of Fox Hunting.

Set to Music by Charles Coote, Esq.

THE morning is breaking, the fog clears away ;
The wind's blowing soft, it's a fine hunting day ;
Capp'd, booted, and spurr'd, and the breakfast well o'er,
The groom leads your cover hack up to the door ;
In health and in spirits you mount on his back,
And canter away to some favourite pack.

Arrived at the "meet," friendly greetings are there ;
Such praising this horse, and admiring that mare ;
Discuss'd are the merits of pig-skin and bit ;
Pocket pistols are primed, and Havannas are lit,
Till the Master (glad sound) says it's time to begin,
When it's "Heigh into cover ! hark over ! yeu in !"

Now, down with cigars, take a pull at your girth,
We're sure of a "find" if there's no open earth ;
Hold hard ! there, you youngster, keep out of that ride,
When hounds are in cover your place is outside.
All is silent as death, save the covert resounds
With the crack of a whip, or a cheer to the hounds.

Loo' in there ! have at him ! yoi, wind him, good lads !
Are sounds very fatal to brushes and pads.
"Hark to, Monarch ! yoi, Fatal ! get to him !" the cry :
"Hi, Bounty ! yoi, Tell Tale ! have at him, old boy !
Be steady, it's right, boys, as sure as we're born,
Tally-ho ! tally-ho ! hark ! there goes the horn !"

A dog fox is running his hardest to find
A place to be safe in ; the pack is behind,
With their heads in the air and their "sterns" drooping
    down,
At a rate that will soon do the cocktails all brown
No bullfinch can frighten or timber appal :
We heed not a damper, nor care for a fall.

The pace is terrific, and burning the scent,
The pack cease their music by common consent,
Except now and then a stray challenge is heard,
The leading hound streaming away like a bird ;
The tailing is awful, as you may expect.
And with "purling" and "pumping" the field gets select.

A good fifty minutes, yet still he's not done,
Pinks call for their second to finish the run ;
Poor Reynard just now, though, has nothing to brag on,
His brush has got daggled, and put him the drag on ;
He plays all he knows, but they race him in view,
And he dies in the open, as "good 'uns" should do.

The huntsman is rating away like a Turk,
He's off and among them, his whip is at work ;
He's lifted poor Charley above his head high.
And "whoo-hoop!" mid the baying of hounds rends the sky
The "bell-pull," as trophy, is kept to preserve,
And the hounds eat the fox they so richly deserve.

Whoo-hoop ! whoo-hoop ! whoo-hoop ! whoo-hoop !
And the hounds eat the fox they so richly deserve

'Tis Past.

"THE LIGHT OF OTHER DAYS."

'Tis past! the maddening dream is o'er,
    That withering word, " Farewell," is spoken,
Whose icy touch hath reached the core
    Of this fond heart — and it is broken.
Henceforth this world is one dark void,
    Yet unkind memory lingers on,
Showing that with my peace destroy'd,
    The sunshine of my life is gone.

The potent lightning's vivid stroke,
    By which the " forest monarch " fell,
Was not more fatal to the oak,
    Than to my heart was that Farewell!
And oh! what torture 'tis to bear,
    When every gleam of hope is gone,
With soul o'ershadowed by despair,
    To feel the curse of loving on!

To-morrow is the food on which procrastination lives:
tis also the day on which idle men work and fools reform!

The Reward.

WRITTEN ON THE DEATH OF A VERY DEAR AND VALUED FRIEND
WHO DIED RICH IN THE FAITH OF "HIM" WHO ALONE
CAN SAVE.

THE soul hath burst its prison bars,
   And left its home of clay,
And journeys on, amid the stars,
   To its glad home away :
Bright angels come in glorious throngs,
   To speed it on its track,
Cheering the way with joyous songs ;
   Oh ! who would wish it back ?

Forgotten now the grief and woes
   It may have suffer'd here ;
On to its resting-place it goes,
   Nor harbours doubt or fear ;
Firm in the faith of God's dear Son,
   (All competent to save)
The soul its blest reward hath gain'd ;
   The body's in the grave.

Our actions should be such only as our enemies would
never allude to !

Up with the Standard of England.

[Inserted by the kind permission of Mr. G. Emery, 408, Oxford Street, London, to whom the Copyright belongs, and where the Music may be had.]

HARK ! hark ! where the lion is roaring ;
 List ! list ! 'tis the growl of the bear,
Above the proud Eagle is soaring,
 The Crescent waves high in the air.
The steed with impatience is neighing,
 The flag of rude War is unfurled,
The Trumpet its wild note is braying,
 And threatens the peace of the World.
   Then up with the Standard of England,
    Our watchword alone be " Advance ! "
   Up, up with the Standard of England
    And raise the brave Banner of France.

'Tis fearful that Life should be wasted,
 'Tis dreadful that Blood should be shed,
That the Horrors of war should be tasted,
 And that Ravens and Wolves should be fed.
All that honour permits has been borne,
 Every mild art of peace has been tried,
Mediation been met with proud scorn,
 And now " War to the knife " must decide.
   Then up with the Standard of England, &c.

Then onward by Sea and by Land,
    Since there's no other course to pursue,
Let old England and France hand in hand,
    Show the world what, combined, they can do ;
Let our scabbardless swords meet the light,
    Down, down with the Tyrant ! our cry,
'Tis for honour and justice we fight,
    So forward ! to conquer or die.
        Then up with the Standard of England, &c.

My Old Wife is a good Old Cratur.

With this, as with everything else that has proceeded from my pen, there was an attendant incident from which it sprung.

Some years ago, I had occasion to cross the moors that lie between Rowsley and Chesterfield. It was in March, and the busy bracing wind was fully engaged in keeping up the character of the month ; it was blowing anyhow, and only as a "high-peak wind, in a passion," knows how to blow, when I saw approaching me a horse and cart, seated in which was a hardy, healthy-looking old couple, that it did one's heart good to look upon. Just before we met, the old man, after doing battle bravely with his hat, which evinced an insane desire to leave his head (I may observe the old lady was driving), he suddenly cried, "Wo! my man !" Now, this was not addressed to me, as you may perhaps imagine it was, there being just then no one else about, but to the old chestnut horse ; his better half—better by, to be sure, by better three quarters—was driving. My man wouldn't answer the "Wo!" given to, so he stopped, and the old lady, for a moment did so secure, ... tying a small handkerchief over the old man's head and underneath his chin, ... restoring their refractory beaver to a proper ... of which ... in the act of turning up his topcoat collar, ... then I had ... to say, "Take care of him, ... night, ...

when, oh! if you had seen the kindly look the old man gave her as he
said to me, in his strong Derbyshire dialect, " Hey, maister, my old
wife's a good old cratur." The words rang upon my ear until I
reached the town of the warped steeple, and there, procuring writing
materials, I concocted the following song, which has been set to music
by G. Simpson, Sen., and may be had of Messrs. D'Almaine & Co.,
London.

My old wife is a good old cratur,
    Never was a kinder born,
Never did nothing to make me hate her,
    Since the wedding ring she's worn.
        And every morning for my breakfast
            She gives me good toast and roll
        My old wife's a good old cratur,
            My old wife's a good old soul.

Then at night when work is over,
    She brings my bacca and my beer,
So you see, I lives in clover,
    Ain't my wife a good old dear ?
        And every morning for my breakfast, &c.

And when matters run three-cornered,
    She sidles up so droll and kind,
Gives me a "buss" and gently whispers,
    Did 'um vex it ! Never mind.
        And every morning for my breakfast, &c.

If, as now and then it happens,
    I get beery, even then
She never says a cross word to me,
    But welcomes me with, Well done, Ben !
        And every morning for my breakfast, &c.

Some folks live in better houses,
    Some folks live on daintier cheer,
But none of them have got such spouses,
    Nor such bacca nor such beer.
      And every morning for my breakfast, &c.

Blest with health and my old cratur,
    From all feuds and discord free,
I'm quite convinced throughout all nature
    There ain't a happier chap than me.
      'Cos every morning for my breakfast, &c.

Lines to my Bulldog.

ON BEING ADVISED TO GET RID OF A VERY PERFECT SPECIMEN, THEN IN MY POSSESSION.

I LOVE thee, Rattler, for thine honest heart,
And 'gainst traducers gladly take thy part :
Thou'rt faithful, Rattler ; no time-serving friend,
But lovest (once loving) truly to the end.
A change of fortune makes no change in thee,
(Which 'mong our biped friends we often see) ;
Watchful as ever of thy master's weal ;
Warm, too, as ever is the love you feel.
The worst thing 'gainst thee I have yet heard said,
Is, thou hast gotten a true bulldog's head ;
But tell them, Rattler, ere we two shall part,
They first must prove thou lack'st a bulldog's heart :
Till then, my canine friend, I'll love thee still.
Let a fastidious world say whatsoe'er it will.

G

Old Morton, the Miller.

OLD MORTON, the miller, was turned of threescore,
  Yet he laughed with a feeling of pride,
As he thought he had only to wait one week more,
  And young Patty would then be his bride;
He had spoken her parents, they gave their consent,
  For old Morton, the miller, had gold;
How often have parents to sigh and repent,
  Over some young warm heart they have sold!
    Old men, old men, list to my lay,
    Hearts like young Patty's are given away ;
    Old men, old men, need ye be told,
    Cupid, sly urchin, but laughs at your gold!

Poor Patty, once cheerful, light-hearted and gay,
  Now lonely, dejected, and pale,
As she ever had been since a youth went away,
  Whose death she was taught to bewail;
But the Fates, predetermined these two should not part,
  With glory her soldier brought back ;
She gave to her hero her hand and her heart,
  And gave Morton, the miller, the sack.
    Old men, old men, list to my lay, &c.

IN making our arrangements to live, we should never
forget that we have also to die.

The King of Terrors.

WRITTEN ON LEARNING THAT HIS ROYAL HIGHNESS PRINCE
ALBERT HAD DEPARTED TO THE BETTER LAND.

STEALTHY thy footsteps, silent thy tread,
And fearful thy coming, great King of the Dead :
No ! no ! that's a title too lofty for thee,
Resistless, remorseless, and dread though ye be.
Thou art King of the Living, insatiate Death ;
Thou hast power o'er the pulse, o'er the heart, and the
        breath ;
But that once departed thy tyranny's o'er ;
Thou hast kill'd, thou hast conquer'd, thou canst do
        no more.

Thy master, grim tyrant, the Lord o'er the grave,
Stands anxiously waiting the freed soul to save ;
Thou combat'st the body, the soul soars above,
On the firm wings of Faith to the mansions of love :
Forgiveness, and pity, where Jesus, its Friend
Bids it welcome to peace and to joy without end.
Then let us so live that when Death shall appear,
We may bow to his sceptre without any fear.

THE tear of pity is a distillation of the soul, and bears a
heavenly quality about it.

Forget Him!

PUBLISHED AS A SONG IN 1846.

[Music by George Simpson, Jun.]

FORGET him!   Oh, how little they
  Who counsel thus can know the feeling
Which graved his image on this heart,
  And through its inmost core is stealing.

Forget him!   They have never felt
  The wild and throbbing pulse which tells
Where Love hath o'erturned Reason's throne,
  And monarch of the bosom dwells.

Forget him!   Yes, should madness pluck
  Fond memory from this tortured brain,
Perchance, in mental darkness lost,
  The vision ne'er may come again.

But while, as now, each varied sense,
  True to its idol worships on,
This faithful heart shall be its shrine
  When every other feeling's gone.

The Gipsy Mother.

[Music by Stephen Glover.   Published by, and may be had of,
Mr. Harrison, Music Depôt, Birmingham.]

SHE sat the statue of despair ;
Her silken, black, disheveled hair
In wild disorder hung, while she
Bowed 'neath her load of misery.
Her deeply dark, yet tearless eye
Was prayer-like lifted to the sky,
As she, in piteous accents wild,
Bewailed her dying vagrant child.

It was a gipsy's form and face
Who, in that wild and lonely place,
Had sat her down in madness, o'er
The fever'd creature that she bore.
Oh ! 'twas a saddening sight to see
The mother's yearning agony,
As she, in piteous accents wild,
Bewailed her dying vagrant child.

And see ! she clasps with trembling arm,
In maniac hope to keep it warm,
The babe that ne'er again may stir,
And yet that babe was all ʼ ʼ ʼ
Where be her kindred ?   Where its sire,
To soothe her blighted brain of fire ?
Heard ye that piercing outcry wild ʼ
She knows 'tis dead — that gipsy child !

The Legend of Nettleford.

A GHOST STORY.

Being a full, true, and faithful account of a dread and fearful ap-
parition, which for a length of time served to horrify and "fright
from its propriety," that otherwise very quiet and peaceful village;
together with a correct and detailed narrative of the startling and
truly appalling consequences which grew out of, and were attendant
upon, the wild and reckless daring of one Anthony Crump, of that
ilk, the which ill-advised temerity, and ungovernable spirit of adventure, he (the said Anthony) still lives bitterly to deplore.

THE village of Nettleford long hath been known
As having a fine Norman church of its own,
And a castle in ruins, though some folks declare
That the ruins are terribly out of repair ;
     Be that as it may,
     There is one thing to say,
You don't see such ruins, mind, every day.

'Bout a mile from the castle, near Cossington Wood,
Is the site where an old Roman monastery stood ;
And, cover'd all over with blackthorns and briars,
Is the place where they buried the monks and the friars ;
     And there is not a doubt
     (From what I can make out
While they lived, they lived well, and got awfully stout.

If you turn to the right, and keep on half a mile,
Down the Bleeding Oak Lane, you will come to a stile,
Which, when you 've got over (right easy to do),
A black and white half-timber'd house meets your view :

> That is Clapperton Grange,
> And 'twas there that a strange

And terrible spectre at night used to range.

Yes, here did a ghost walk, and always at night ;
And always by moonlight, and always in white ;
Besides, it walked lame, the which proved beyond doubt
'Twas the ghost of some person who died of the gout,

> On which murmurers said,
> With a shake of the head,

"Blair's gout pills were fine, but they 'd not cure the dead."

The oldest inhabitant, nicknamed "Deaf Daniel,"
Remembered a man with his legs wrapped in flannel,
Who once lived at the Grange ; and could further remember

> That he died very rich, and he died in December.
> It was he, that was plain,
> And he 'd come back again,

To look after some gold that he hid in a drain.

The Grange now stood empty, and had done for years ;
Some deterr'd by high rental, and some by their fears ;
Its last tenant, Job Spinks, long ago, it was said,
Saw the ghost, when at once in wild terror he fled ;

> And so anxious was he
> From the ghost to get free,

That he ne'er paid his rent—but that's nothing to me

The matter at length grew decidedly serious,
It frightened Mark Mobbs till he went quite delirious,
Though some people say, and a many folks think,
That it was not so much the alarm as the drink !
   But the bravest and best
   Who by daylight would jest,
After dark were as timid and alarmed as the rest.

And so it became quite the country's talk,
For no end of people had seen the ghost walk ;
There were Rogers and Martin, Bill Gibbs and George Gore,
Besides Philip Parslow, who 'd seen it before !
   So the villagers met
   To see how they might get
Out of what hurt them worse than the National Debt.

Now whoever knows Nettleford knows the "Three Crowns,"
Nearly opposite Frampton's, and next door to Brown's ;
And just round the corner, three doors from the pump,
Lives the pride of old Nettleford, Anthony Crump ;
   In stature but small,
   But that 's nothing at all,
For the greatest hearts often to little folks fall.

The meeting was crowded, and Anthony there ;
Bob Belthard, the blacksmith, was called to the chair,
Who took it, and stated for why they 'd assembled,
At which more than one in the company trembled ;
   Says Belthard, says he,
   " If I might make so free,
I consider all ghosts as mere fiddle-de-doo."

"What are taken," says Belthard, "for spirits and ghosts,
For the most part turn out either donkeys or posts,
Or some fool with a sheet on; this Grange ghost you'll see
Is all "bosh," as I'll prove, if you'll leave it to me."
But the villagers said,
As they listen'd with dread,
They didn't think Belthard was right in his head.

Still Belthard continued, "Is any one here
Whose heart, like my own, is a stranger to fear?
Let him hold his right hand up." Cried Crump, "Look at me!
And the man you inquire for at once you shall see."
"Hurrah!" cried the smith,
"He's a real bit of pith,
And precisely the man I should like to go with."

The meeting was frantic with joy as they gazed
On these two noble spirits, but most were amazed
At the courage evinced by brave Anthony Crump,
Who lived round the corner, three doors from the pump;
He, majestic and stern,
Said to Belthard, "I burn
With desire to watch singly; come, give me first turn."

"You're on!" said the blacksmith; "this evening, alone,
To the ghost and the village your pluck shall be shown."
"I don't know about that," said brave Crump; "how's the
moon?
Don't you fancy to-night would be RATHER TOO SOON?"
But the meeting cried, "No!
It's the right time to go,
And you're certain to see him." Crump merely said "Oh!"

The party broke up, and the village was glad,
And said what a nice pleasant meeting they'd had;
That Crump was a "brick," and they always had known it;
And as to "white feather," he never had shown it.

  While this clamour went on,
  Where is Anthony gone?
Towards home to think over the blacksmith's "You're on!"

How many a man, in the heat of debate,
Has uttered some words he repented too late;
So Anthony now, when his spirit got cool,
Had a kind of a notion he'd acted the fool.

  He felt sorely dismay'd
  At the promise he'd made,
And, if truth must be spoken, was rather afraid.

  The wild excitement of the hour
  Was losing fast its hold and power;
   And Crump now thought
  That village honours, local fame,
  And even Valour's courted name,
   Were dearly bought

  By reckless deeds and bold exploits,
  (As meeting ghosts on moonlight nights),
   And he could see
  That lots of people could be found,
  Who dwelt within the church bells' sound,
   More fit than he

For such encounters ; and 'twas plain
The meeting should be call'd again,
    To reconsider
His proposition : " For," said he,
" My children fatherless may be —
    My wife a 'widder.' "

Thus did his martial soul recoil :
But only, mark ye, for a while :
    For Courage now
Came to the rescue, and exclaimed,
"Shall Crump of Nettleford be shamed,
    Or break his vow ?"

" Rather than that," brave Crump replies,
" Come all the ghosts before my eyes
    That ever haunted
This wicked world since it was made :
I say again, Let all parade,
    I 'll not be daunted."

To the wife of his bosom, he next wends his way,
With a kind of misgiving as to what she might say,
For Matilda, his uxor, as often we find,
Had a way, as she called it, of " speaking her mind !"
    When she saw with affright,
    That her husband looked white,
She said, "Anthony Crump, you have been and got 'tight.'"

"Matilda," he said, in a dolorous tone,
"I am going to the Grange, love, and going alone,
To dispose of the question, and that on the spot,
Whether what haunts the Grange is a real ghost or not."
   His wife, with asperity, answered him thus,
   "I don't see at all that it matters to us
   If the ghost that you speak of is false or is true,
   Though it's haunting the Grange, man, it doesn't
    haunt you."

"What you say, my Matilda, no doubt is a fact,
But I've given my word, and I cannot retract.
Should I fall, as I may do—for Fate has no rule—
Send Ann to her aunt's, and let Bob go to school.
   Now, leave me my darling," he said, with a smile,
   I wish to think o'er my affairs for awhile;
   Oh, Matilda, remember, I've not made my will,
   But it doesn't much matter, as my property's nil."

Wives are obedient creatures ever,
Contradicting husbands never.
So his rib went off, as she was told,
Saying, "Ah! you'll catch a pretty cold."

Crump, to his thoughts thus left alone,
(What those thoughts were shall ne'er be known),
Did what I think you'll all admire,
Lighted his pipe, and raked the fire;
   Ensconced him in his old arm chair,
   Drew his lean fingers through his hair,
   Took at the glowing bars a stare,
   And hoped the ghost would not be there.

He muses, sleeps, and dreams that he
Nine mortal ghosts at once can see,
Some tall, some short, some stout, some slim,
And all with sticks, approaching him ;
        They strike, and loud doth bold Crump scream,
        And wakes to find it was a dream ;
        His wife calls out, " Why, Crump, 's that you ?
        Come up to bed, you stupid, do !"

But part, from out the old church tower,
The clock tells forth the midnight hour :
            'Tis twelve o'clock,
Which hearing, Anthony did start,
And 'gainst his ribs his noble heart
            Did bump and knock :

As to the door his neighbours came,
Calling the valiant Crump by name ;
            "'Tis time for starting !"
List to that wild exulting shout !
The noble Anthony turns out ;
            And now they 're parting.

Said Anthony, " My valued friends,
Howe'er this night's adventure ends,
            Which perhaps may sever
Myself and you for evermore.
You will not follow, I implore ;"
            They all said, " Never !"

To each of this devoted band
He bids farewell, and gives his hand,
  Then wends his way ;
And as his form fades from their sight,
Towards the Grange, they shout "Good-night !"
  And then, " Hooray !"

Not Quixote, when knighted, or Sancho, his squire,
E'er felt for adventure their hearts beating higher
Than did Anthony now, save alack ! and alack !
A burning desire to turn round and go back.
  And a man must be bold
  Who turns out in the cold,
To look out for a ghost which he's bound to behold.

One Curtius, a Roman, at least so 'tis said,
Jumped down a vast chasm, which closed o'er his head ;
But the leap that he took down that yawning abyss,
(As a daring exploit), was as nothing to this.
  For no one would dare,
  I should think, to compare
  The Roman's rash jump
  To the daring of Crump ;
  Besides people say,
  And maintain to this day,
"'Twas no credit to Curtius ; for his horse ran away."

A man's not expected to go his best pace
When he has to meet danger, and that face to face ;
And the ghost Crump might meet would, for all he knew,
  take him,

And double him up, and ANOTHER GHOST make him ;
  So he walked rather slow ;
  Mind you, fair heel and toe,
And quite ready, if called on, to "right about" go.

Thus with care he approaches the Grange, when he hears,
Or fancies he does (for 'tis strange how men's fears
Lend an echo to nothing), a strange sort of noise,
Which rather made Anthony open his eyes ;
  And distinct on his ear
  Sounds of footsteps draw near,
And bold Anthony listens, and trembles with fear.

The object approaches, whatever it be ;
Crump shivers and shakes, and goes weak in the knee ;
The dread sounds get plainer, the footsteps come on ;
Crump's bolted—the Hero of Nettleford's gone !
  We've heard about ghosts, and we've read about others,
  From "Hamlet's papa," to the "Corsican Brothers ;"
  But among all the party, I firmly suspect,
  Not one e'er produced such a startling effect.

Poor Anthony runs till he's clean out of breath ;
'Tis useless disguising, he's frighten'd to death !
And the villagers all, in a body, turn out,
Having heard in the distance Crump's maniac shout.
  Crump was speechless with fear,
  As his neighbours drew near ;
Which beholding, they fled, leaving Crump in the rear.

The village affrighted, uprose as one man,
Got the fire engine out, a most praiseworthy plan ;
And rung the bells backwards, which I don't admire,
As it led to the notion the church was on fire.

In the midst of the row
Came up Belthard, I vow,
Saying, "I've seen the ghost—it's JOE PILKINGTON's COW!

And so it turned out ; the old cow's back was sore
From a hurt she received at Bob Repton's barn door,
And the Cow Leech had plastered the place up quite neat
With some wool, and some pitch, and a piece of old sheet ;

And she, beyond doubt,
It was, wandering about,
Who believers in ghosts had thus put to the rout.

But where is bold Anthony Crump all this while ?
He lies knock'd out of time against Calloway's stile ;
They shake him, and pinch him, but Crump never stirr'd,
Till the blacksmith said, "Crump, it was me that you heard ;"

Then he opened his eyes
With a look of surprise,
Saying, "Honour, now, Belthard ; you're not telling fibs ?"

"Far from it, my friend," replied Belthard ; " I went
Just to see if you really had said what you meant,
And was coming to say so, when, ' Murder !' you cried,
And went off like a racehorse ; that can't be denied."

Neighbour kindness display'd ;
Crump to bed was convey'd,
But I shall not repeat the remarks his wife made.

The joy of the natives was past all belief :
The tidings they heard gave them perfect relief ;
The ghost was a COW ! and, Oh ! glorious reality !
No phantom infested that charming locality.
   But they 'll never have done,
   Who in earnest, or fun
Still chaff Crump with "There 's footsteps ; now, Anthony,
  run !"

MORAL.

DEAR READER, if ever you hear of a ghost,
(And nursemaids and imbeciles talk 'bout them most),
Nip such stories at once in the bud, for you 'll find
They lay terrible hold on the juvenile mind ;
Nor, when they get older, can Reason quite clear
The brain of the poison thus planted by Fear ;
And 'tis strange with what fondness the memory clings
To the morbid enjoyment of unexplained things.

   Then, if true, as folks talk,
   That a ghost can but WALK,
   One has only to RUN,
   Their intention to balk ;
   While there 's not upon record,
   (For all they assert),
   The name of one person
   A ghost ever hurt !

H

A "Samaritan" Ode,

ADDRESSED TO EVERYBODY.

["We regret to learn that poor old Tom Cribb is extremely ill at the
house of his son, at Woolwich."—*Vide* BELL'S LIFE, Jan. 30, 1848.]

Go, gaze on the Champion ! look at him now,
With that pale sunken cheek, and the damp on his brow ;
Compare what he was with what now meets your view—
It will show what "old age" and long illness can do.
Where now is the "giant-like" power of his arm,
That fill'd all the men of his day with alarm ?
Where, where is the muscle that gave that arm strength
To make the huge MOLINEUX measure his length ?
All, all are departed ; the spirit alone
Survives all his physical energies, gone.
There, beaten at last, lies the gamest and best
That ever the "fistic arena" possess'd—
TOM CRIBB (for 'tis you), there 's a charm in thy name,
If true British courage and unsullied fame
Be passport to old English sympathy—then
Not useless shall prove this appeal from my pen.
Neglect shall not chill, nor stern Want ever come,
With their with'ring effect, to the poor "old man's home."
Shall we suffer an honest, brave creature like this
One essential to need, or one comfort to miss ?
No ! with hands ever open, and hearts prone to feel,
All true men their shoulders will put to the wheel.

What is it among us ?   There are lots will be found,
Who, though not in position to fork out a pound,
Will loose with much pleasure a "bull," or a "bob,"
Or a "tizzy," for 'tis but just "bilking" the "gob";
One glass or two less, or some frisk set aside ;
Some little odd pleasure we think of, denied,
And there are at once all the funds we require
For doing an act which e'en angels admire.
So now, let's be "bricks," and at once set about it ;
We can—and, remember, he can't—do without it.
Let each "cadge" a trifle, which by post let him send
To "Bell,"* who is ever the fighting man's friend.
'Tis an act the old Champion will never forget,
And one we shall never have cause to regret.
So thus to a close my long missive I bring,
And am, gentle sirs, an old FARMER from Tring.

* The Editor of *Bell's Life*.

IT is fervently to be desired that mankind were obliged to
make into parcels all, or most of the unmasked advice they
give. Without doubt the cost of the paper and string,
together with the trouble of directing, would put a partial
stop to its indulgence.

𝔐𝔬𝔫𝔬𝔡𝔶 𝔬𝔫 𝔱𝔥𝔢 𝔇𝔢𝔞𝔱𝔥 𝔬𝔣 𝔗𝔬𝔪 𝔆𝔯𝔦𝔟𝔟.

THE struggle 's over, and he sleeps at last ;
His pains, his pleasures, and his sorrow 's past.
Like some huge oak, uprooted by the storm,
Lies the old Champion's cold and senseless form.
Insatiate Death ! throughout thy conquests grim
Thou ne'er didst beat a braver man than him.
Ask those who knew, him if a nobler heart
Was ever "cast" to play a manly part
In this life's drama ?   Mark his vigorous prime,
Ere fell Disease, or more relentless Time
Had laid their heavy hands upon his head,
And his activity and strength were fled ;
How marked by deeds loud heralded by Fame,
Which gave TOM CRIBB the envied Champion's name !
He " fought and conquered ;" but how oft and well,
Let the true page of " Fistiana " tell ;
Only observing, that his laurels gained,
Cowardice ne'er tarnished, nor dishonour stained.
His life was chequered, and the latter part
Bore no comparison to its brighter start !
And but for filial kindness, and a few
Of kindred spirits 'mong the staunch and true,
The fine old man (an undeserved doom)
Had breathed his last 'midst penury's sad gloom.
A shield was formed of good and feeling hearts,

Which warded off Misfortune's stings and darts ,
Mild gentle Pity sought the hero's bed,
And smoothed the pillow for his aching head.
His last hard fight with Death was just the same
As all his others—showed unflinching game ;
Till Nature, who had backed him, went up to him,
(Seeing all chance was gone), and kindly drew him.
And now let 's rear a tablet o'er his grave,
To show how Englishmen respect the brave.
No costly marble, nor letter-gilded stone —
Leave such distinction to the rich alone !
Let some plain slab record his age and name.
And leave the rest to History and Fame.

Monody on Grace Darling.

'TWERE impious to weep, the gentle maiden dead :
Let not one tear of selfish love be shed,
Nor dare repine that Providence denies
A longer absence from her native skies.
It was a mighty mission, which complete,
Her happy spirit takes its well-earned seat
At His right hand, who practises alone
A more extended mercy than her own.
Happy thy lot, dear Grace, for whom it was decreed
To crowd a life of virtue into one immortal deed.

Success to Thee, Old England.

HERE's success to thee, Old England,
  Success to thee, and then
A health to those brave sons of thine,
  The gallant Englishmen.
For warmer hearts have never throbb'd,
  Nor braver ever been,
Than those who form, in phalanx warm,
  The bulwark of thy Queen.

Then success to thee, Old England,
  For whate'er thy errors be,
Thou still art known from zone to zone,
  As the dauntless and the free.
And who but thee, Old England,
  Thou merciful as brave,
Performed that heavenly mission
  Which gave freedom to the slave ?

So success to thee, Old England,
  Who 'mong thy blessings rare,
Gives as a toast (proud Briton's boast),
  Thy " bright-eyed daughters fair !"
And should oppressive foemen dare
  'Gainst thee to lift a hand,
Thy sons shall show the love they owe
  To thee, their native land ?

The Passing Bell.

HARK! where the Passing Bell, with mournful tone,
Tells that again the tyrant's work is done :
Another victim to stern Fate's decree,
Has met a doom fast hurrying on towards thee !
Prepare to meet it, for no earthly power
May set aside that doom for one brief hour :
Slowly, perchance, but surely, on it comes,
Beckoning creation to their long, last homes !
Yet comes undreaded by the well-schooled soul,
Who holds it harbinger of that blest goal,
The glad abode of HIM whose perfect love
Awaits the souls of faithful ones above.
Strong in belief of HIM who died to save,
The trusting Christian smiling meets his grave.

Turn, then, Oh ! turn to HIM who alone hath power to give
An angel's courage when you die, and peace while yet you live.
In meekness bend thy knee : commence the needful task ;
Beg heaven's pardon for your sins, WHILE YOU HAVE STRENGTH
    TO ASK !

How frequently in marriage, as in the game of "blind man's buff," a totally different person is caught to what was either expected or desired : while in' neither case (unfortunately) is the bandage removed until it is too late to repair the error committed.

They found a Friend.

THE north wind chaunts his wildest song,
The leafless forest boughs among,
Dark night hath drawn her mantle o'er
The barren waste and trackless moor,
There wandering, shivering, side by side
Stern Want their sad and only guide,
Without one earthly friend or home,
The children of the pauper roam.
The boy, with gentle accents, said,
(Patting his little sister's head) —
" Don't cry, dear Anna ; dry that tear ;
None but the wicked need to fear ;
Bright morn will soon be here, and then
We 're sure to meet some friend again !"
Each word prophetic that he said,
Bright morning came — it found them dead !
Their earthly troubles at an end ;
The child was right — they found a Friend.

UNPRETENDED love, disinterested friendship, political
honesty, and tortoiseshell tom cats, are four things rarely
to be met with.

Gold, Mighty Gold!

Hurrah ! for the most potent monarch on earth,
Who hath reigned in his might since the hour of his birth ,
Whose standard is followed where'er 'tis unfurled,
And whose empire extendeth all over the world :
All, all are his subjects, the young and the old —
And the monarch I sing of is Gold, mighty Gold !

The soldier, when fighting for honour and fame,
Will strike yet the fiercer at sound of his name :
While the love-smile of woman (to all justly dear),
Beams brighter by far if the Monarch draws near :
E'en the heart of the miser, though flinty and cold,
Will warm into rapture at sight of King Gold.

Alike are his vassals — the wise man and fool —
Each bows and submits with delight to his rule ;
In his ranks, too, are number'd the slave and the free :
Then say — Are there any as potent as he ?
Obey'd are his mandates in hot climes as cold ;
Then hurrah ! for the ruler of monarchs — King Gold !

The friends of a prosperous man, like the leaves of the summer tree, are many. Anon the winter of misfortune comes, and lo ! the leaves fall off !

The Norton Elm.

[Upon the Green, in the centre of the town of Chipping Norton, for
two centuries at least, had stood a wide-spreading colossal Elm Tree;
a market hall being held desirable, it was, by the "powers that be,"
decided to have the old tree cut down, and the present glorious
structure erected on the spot where it stood.]

Two HUNDRED years at least, had seen
That Monarch Elm on Norton Green;
The noisy rooks, its boughs among,
Had built their nests, and rear'd their young:
The sparrows claimed a vested right
To chirrup on its topmost height;
The starling, in its hollow arm,
Had built for years its nest so warm.
(Though, lying useless, all around
Was lots of fitting vacant ground),
The poor old tree was doomed to fall,
And rooks and starlings banished all.
It was a pity, for that fine old tree
Formed part of Norton's history.
Grey-headed men would speak, with glee,
Of boyhood's sports beneath that tree:
And crones, grown garrulous, would tell
How early swains had tried to spell
Their rude initials on its bark,
And show, or try to show, the mark.
Could it have told—that Nature's child,

The stories true, and legends wild :
The many changes, bad and good,
That had occurred, since there it stood,
'Twould form a chronicle to read,
Strange, very, very strange indeed.
The spoiler came in evil hour,
Who lacking taste, and having power,
O monstrous act ! decreed its fall,
And built the present Market Hall.

The Alarm.

STARTING from troubled sleep, in wild affright,
What piercing screams disturb the peaceful night ?
List ! 'tis a smother'd cry salutes mine ear,
And now a stifled groan begets new fear :
I hear strange voices, and the hurrying tread
Of many people : hark ! they say " He 's dead '"
The gleam of crackling fire, with glare around,
Adds to the horror of each dreadful sound.
They call for water !—I can bear no more ;
Cold perspiration starts from every pore !
With frenzied haste the window up I threw ;
A half-scorched body met my sickening view.
The truth revealing ; quick I turned away—
Our neighbour Perkins killed his pig that day !

Wife of my Bosom.

[THE MARINER'S SONG.]

WIFE of my bosom ! my soul's dearest treasure,
  Star of my dwelling-place, listen to me ;
Know that when absent, my only true pleasure
  Is thinking, dear Mary, of home and of thee !
And when in his fury the Storm King was riding
  The wild waves that foamed as he hurried them on,
And the thunder, awoke in his anger, was chiding
  And all light, save the vivid forked lightning, was gone.

When Despair laid his hand on the heart of the boldest,
  Stern Misery whispered her tale in each ear ;
When Hope scarcely spoke, and in tones of the coldest,
  And each one on board was the vassal of fear.
I had, in that hour of dark peril, a feeling,
  Which never forsakes me, where'er I may be,
The glow of affection around my heart stealing,
  Fondly telling, dear Mary, of home and of thee.

EPITAPH ON A DRUNKARD. — Here lieth the body of one,
who for many years waged an unequal contest with the wine
cup, until Nature—his best friend and backer—seeing he
only stood up to be punished, without a chance to win,
kindly threw up the sponge.

Old Fashioned Times.

In old fashioned times, when the old fashioned folk,
    With their friends and relations around,
Would welcome old Christmas with dance, song, and joke,
    And the fiddle's good old fashioned sound.
The old paneled parlour was put in request,
    The holly and ivy were there ;
And neighbour met neighbour, decked out in their best,
    To partake of the old fashioned fare.

No cards were then printed, with formal invite,
    Nor pink scented paper, with some
Expression of MAMMA's or PAPA's delight ;
    They asked you, and MEANT you to come.
Then the old fashioned shake of the hand which they gave,
    With the welcome that shone in their smile,
And the honest "how are you ? I hope you are brave,"
    For THAT was the old fashioned style !

While the old-fashioned country dance would enlist
    The young to enjoy its delight,
The old folks sat down to a rubber at whist,
    And so passed the old Christmas night.
The mistletoe bough to the ceiling was hung,
    Old excuse for the innocent kiss,
Nor Prudery's self would pronounce it as wrong
    On a joyous occasion like this.

Each house had its party, each party was gay ;
   Good Nature and Cheerfulness lent
Their aid to induce you to lengthen your stay,
   And Regret only came when you went.
Those, those were the times, let them talk as they may,
   When folks met to be happy and free !
'Tis a pity such customs should e'er pass away,
   However OLD FASHIONED THEY BE !

A Day at Binton's Farm.

[IT were no book of mine did it not contain some allusion to the noble
art of "rat catching." The subjoined effusion being in as mild a form
as any thing I have ever penned on that subject, I am induced to
insert it.]

FARMER BINTON had written Ned Perkins to say
That he purposed on Friday to thrash out a bay ;
That he'd sent to George Haynes about ferrets, and so
They expected on Friday to have a grand go.
The morning is come, the machine got in motion,
(Which rather beats thrashing by hand, I've a notion) ;
The chaff in a simoom of dust floats along,
And the team do their work to the wagoner's song.
George's outposts well guarded, the shindy begins,
At the expense of rats' lives and the countrymen's shins.
" Don't trample the wheat out," says Binton, " I pray ;
There's no sort of hurry— they can't get away."

"There's one where that dog is—he's shifted—ne'er mind.
They'll all be crept into one corner, you'll find.
Halloo! there's a great 'un! hie, Tartar! good lad—
He's got him. Look yonder—they're bolting like mad."
My soul, there's a scuffle. "Be careful, I begs—
You'll have those fork-tines into somebody's legs!"
"Look out, Mr. Binton; there's one at your back,
On the top of the chaff-hole—just give him a crack."
"Mind, mind where you're hitting—there's one up the wall."
"Oh! I thought it a mouse by its being so small."
"No, no, it's a rat, look—and here are the rest—
There's eight or nine more of 'em down in this nest."
They are nearing the bottom—each sheaf they displace
Yields a rat, which produces a kill or a race.
"Good Tartar! hie Nettle! dead, dead!—Pincher, drop it."
"There's one up the wall again—Petipher, stop it."
"Now, clumsy!—he's miss'd him!" Oh, he's safe enough:
He's popp'd through that air hole and into the sough."
"Bill Hawkins, run round, lad, and look out a bit—
They're all sure to make for the "kid pile" or "pit."
The bay is alive with them—hark! what a row, sirs;
A young one has crept up Jack Morris's trowsers,
Who pale with affright, and exerting his muscle,
Belabours the place where a maid ties her bustle.
And thus they kept shouting and whacking away,
Till at last they got down to the floor of the bay,
Where full thirty old ones—'tis true, on my soul—
Were found (as is often the case) in one hole.
And then, such an uproar when they were got out,
Such shouting and barking, and running about;

All, all, save an old one, were fated to die,
Bill Stokes caught Joe Foster a whack on the eye.
Thus ended the warfare ! Full ninety had died,
Without counting seven they'd topper'd outside :
When, finding no others were left them to munch,
They left off, and went into Binton's to lunch.

The Ranger.

[This song is an attempt to describe a few of the leading points in the
character of the late Mr. John Penson, Park-keeper, at Trentham Hall,
Staffordshire, whose family have had the honour of serving in that
capacity since the reign of Elizabeth.]

TUNE—"THE FINE OLD ENGLISH GENTLEMAN."

I'll try to paint a portrait, if you'll listen to my lay,
Of a fine old English specimen, whose locks are silvery grey ;
Yet still as young at heart he is—that heart's as free from
  gall,
And he's fond of sport of any sort—as the youngest 'mong
  them all ;
He's a fine old English Forester, one of the olden time.

In days of old, when " LEVISON," the noble and the brave,
An Admiral, bore the British flag triumphant o'er the wave ;
As faithful follower was found a " PENSON " in his pay,
From whom descends " the Forester " we sing about to-day.
He's a fine old English Forester, one of the olden time.

The tuneful lark's gay matin song his early summons sounds,
Then lustily he wends his way o'er Trentham's spacious grounds;
Or mounted, or on foot, he hies around its princely park,
And every person that he meets gets some unique remark
From this fine old English Forester, one of the olden time.

Hark! the unerring rifle's ring, the fatal bullet's sped;
The forest's antler'd monarch dies—a hole drill'd through
　　　his head.
In all pertains to woodcraft's art inferior he's to none;
Few, few can kill a buck like he, or carve him when 'tis done,
He's a fine old English Forester, one of the olden time.

Anon, for orders at the Hall, "the Ranger" may be seen,
As spruce as modern dandy, in his suit of Lincoln green;
And should his noble "Mistress" depart the place that day,
He proudly leads the cavalcade into the Queen's highway.
He's a fine old English Forester, one of the olden time.

And when the boundary is gain'd the Ranger makes his bow,
A very ranger-like "salaam," concocted long ago;
Then blows that note peculiar (a proof his lungs are good),
And this evergreen trots back again to his "cottage near the
　　　wood."
He's a fine old English Forester, one of the olden time.

There are two great points about him that prove him
　　　thorough bred:
His lofty hairless temples, and his fine old chiselled head;
I fancy Deerhound's by his side: and mounted on his "Roan,"
I see him now! O long may Death leave his warm heart alone,
For he's a fine old English Forester, one of the olden time.

I

A Coursing Song.

RESPECTFULLY DEDICATED TO ALL TRUE LOVERS OF THE LEASH.

LET dukes keep their racers, my lord have his stud,
And the squire sport his pack, and his prime bit of blood,
Give me a good kennel of greyhounds, and let
The BEST dog always win, when for coursing we 're met.
  Singing, gently, so ho! halloo! let 'em go,
  There 's no better sport than good coursing can show.

See! stripped of their clothing, look, look! what a treat ;
What muscular haunches, what small cat-like feet ;
With a tail like a rat, and an eye like gazelle,
Long necked and deep chested, they 're safe to run well.
  Singing gently, &c.

Come, where is your starter ? Your judge, where is he ?
Put a brace into slips, and some sport you shall see ;
Hold hard! there, you horsemen! don't ride o'er the ground;
I ne'er saw this beaten but "pussy" was found.
  Singing gently, &c.

So ho! there! I told you ; now, give her fair play ;
It shall all be fair coursing ; no murder to-day ;
The hares, perhaps in weight may have lost half an ounce,
But after this frost you'll just see how they'll bounce.
  Singing gently, &c.

They're running like wildfire ; the black dog's a turn ;
Now the blue 'un's a go-by—she's off for the fern ;
He has thrown, and has miss'd her ; the black dog is in ;
He's a mortal good judge that can tell which will win.
   Singing gently, &c.

The black dog is leading the blue dog a nose ;
She makes for the spinney—my heart, how she goes ;
Th' black dog a thousand ! A-done, sir—a-done !
He has her ! he hasn't ! my soul, what a run !
   Singing gently, &c.

They're getting the slows on, they're all of them beat ;
It's rarely a sportsman enjoys such a treat.
Now, Topper ! now, Bugle ! they'll kill her !—they won't ;
They have her !—they haven't !—she beats 'em—she don't !
   Singing gently, &c.

See, the judge takes his hat off, as he sits on his horse,
And so UNDECIDED's this wonderful course ;
They've managed to kill her, but no man can tell
Which won it, they both ran so HONEST and WELL !
   Singing gently, &c.

Come, fill up your glasses, whatever you drink,
(I shall deem him a "mull" who endeavours to slink),
Here's success to the "long tails," their owners, and all
Who are fond of the sport, whether great folks or small.
   Singing gently, &c.

HYPOCRISY is a masquerade dress lent by the devil, which
will be expected to be personally returned by the wearer.

Donald Gore.

"Don't bother me," says Kate, says she,
　　"Nor teaze me any more;
For, truth to speak, my heart will break,
　　And all for Donald Gore;
While he's away I can't be gay,
　　And smile and laugh like you;
May ill befall me once for all
　　If e'er I prove untrue.

"The birds sing sweetly on each tree,
　　The sun is shining bright;
All happy be, except poor me,
　　With whom 'tis ever night.
Oh! Donald Gore, dear Donald Gore,
　　For thee it is I pine!
There's not a feeling in my heart
　　But what is wholly thine.

"They tell me I do wrong to grieve
　　For one who's lost to me;
But Oh! I never can believe
　　'Tis wrong thus loving thee!
And still through life I'll love with truth,
　　Whatever may befall;
And when I die, thy form, dear youth,
　　Shall fade the last of all.

"The Test Act."

WOULD you the flower of friendship blight,
  Or of its beauty dock it,
The blow need be but very light,
  Just hit the breeches pocket.

Friendship's a pure and holy thing,
  And in men's hearts we lock it ;
Whilst often, mind, the secret spring
  Lies in the breeches pocket.

Friendship shall bring you many friends,
  Pray, therefore do not mock it ;
But would you know how all this ends,
  Just touch the breeches pocket.

The human breast is Friendship's hive,
  With bees of love go stock it ;
But oh ! if you would have them thrive
  Don't touch the breeches pocket.

BOOKS to mankind are as the flowers to the bee. Read,
therefore, I conjure ye ; read ! seeing that the spring and
summer of your life is the proper season for laying in an
useful stock of knowledge, which to the mind, like the well-
stored hive to the bee, is a source of sustenance, when the
dreary winter of old age sets in.

The Confession.

I HAVE long determined that I would, at some period or other (as the only possible atonement now in my power), divulge to the public the dreadful secret contained in the following confession :—

Years of overwhelming grief and unmitigated misery, have entirely failed in at all assuaging the bitter regrets of this crime tortured bosom.

Those who have been much in my society, cannot have failed to notice the frequent fits of melancholy abstraction to which I am subject. The following painful disclosures will at once serve to elucidate the retributive nature of these visitations.

And oh, my very soul sickens when I think how many, whom I have been proud to consider as my friends, will shudder when they ascertain that this hand, which they in the kindness of their hearts have so warmly pressed, has been stained with ——. But I will not anticipate—

It was a damp, cold, foggy, drizzly night,
The moon half gave, and half withheld, her light ;
The hour, approaching twelve ; the month, November ;
And, though 'tis years a-gone, I still remember
The fearful doings of that night as well
As though 'twere yesterday on which it fell.
Its bare remembrance makes my blood run cold,
But conscience dictates, and it SHALL BE TOLD !
Oh ! would in mercy this poor brain were freed
From recollection of that horrid deed !

I've said 'twas night, returning from a friend's,
(So ever joy with some sad sorrow blends).
We had been spending a gay, happy night.
My head, my heart, my pockets, all were light.
Prudence had whisper'd of the coming day,
And so, unknown to all, I stole away ;
My gun —(I had been shooting on that day —
Would it had been ten thousand miles away),
I CARRIED LOADED ! oh, most dire mishap,
That e'er I made in Foden's fence a gap.
To make the distance less, my way I took
Over the fields, by way of Brockley's brook ;
When crossing Vincent's close, before me stood,
Between the Gibbet Lane and Wadley's wood,
The figure of a man !— his outstretched arms
To intercept me, raised my worst alarms.
Behind me, too, quick hurrying steps came on,
I felt all hope of an escape was gone ;
What fiend impelled — what monster coined the thought ?
Enough to tell — the fatal gun I caught,
Raised to my shoulder, and — my eyeballs start —
I fired the murderous charge RIGHT THROUGH HIS HEART !
As I supposed ; but truth demands these words —
It was a SCARECROW, set to frighten birds !
The coming steps I'd heard, with shame I must confess,
Were Allen's drunken cowman's — neither more nor less,
Who having joined me, said, as homeward we were walking,
"I say, what made you shoot at Mr. Vincent's mawkin ?"

Adieu to 1844.

WRITTEN DECEMBER 31ST, AT ELEVEN O'CLOCK, P.M.

AND thou art off, old Forty-four,
　　With all thy good and ill attending,
To join thy kindred gone before,
　　And add to the eternal blending.
What varied scenes of grief and joy
　　Hast thou, old year, been at the making ;
What myriads sent to sleep, old boy,
　　To 'bide the last trump's awful waking ?

What thousands thou hast usher'd in
　　To this sad world of guilt and sorrow ;
But whatsoe'er thy faults have been,
　　Thy reign, old boy, will end to-morrow.
So part we friends, for thou hast dried
　　The tear from many a weeping eye ;
And thy successor, when he's tried
　　May perhaps be worse —and so, good-bye !

———

SIGNIFICANT.—Anybody will lend you an umbrella when it doesn't rain.

———

THEY do things well, who never try ;
Right clever folks, those standers-by !

Empromptu.

WRITTEN ON VIEWING THE BODY OF A YOUNG MAN WHO WAS
KILLED BY LIGHTNING, AT CHARLBURY, OXFORDSHIRE,
JULY 19, 1844.

AND he is dead; aye, dead and cold, and motionless, who but
an hour agone was full of lusty life, of youth and vigour;
whose warm heart's blood ran gaily dancing through a giant
frame; whose stalwart build might almost mock at Time,
and, in its seeming strength, defy disease. And now, behold!
a few brief moments gone, a clammy, ghastly corpse is all
remains!

Look on, I pray you all, and ponder well, this "stern
monument" of LIFE'S UNCERTAINTY!

THERE are some dispositions so palpably and really supe-
rior to others, as to induce the belief, that Nature, in her
manufacture of them, had thrown in a dash of the angel
by way of a finish; while, in contradistinction, others there
are, which seem to be made up of the mere sweepings and
scrapings of the manufactory.

—

VIRTUE in a woman, as the kernel to the nut, gives value,
without which both are worthless.

First Throb of Love.

THE first throb of love this fond heart ever knew,
    Was implanted, dear Mary, by thee ;
And time serves to show me how lasting and true
    That first love, dear Mary, shall be.

Though distance may part us, thy memory still
    I 'll treasure as miser his gold ;
Nor e'er for a moment forget thee, until
    This now beating heart shall be cold.

Whatever awaits me through life's changing scene,
    Wherever on earth I may range,
My constant companion throughout will have been
    A feeling that never can change.

And so will I love thee, unalter'd, till death
    Shall bid me the passion resign ;
One name, fondly whisper'd, shall claim my last breath,
    And, Mary, that name shall be THINE !

A BLACKGUARD is a living syringe, filled with dirty water,
with which he ever and anon doth defile his betters.

A MAN should never think once ere he performs a good
action ; but a thousand times before he does a bad one !

The British Volunteers.

[Written on the Eve of the Russian War, when our brave fellows were so gloriously volunteering for foreign service. The Music may be had at Messrs. Sabin's, Bull Street, Birmingham.]

For a time I've lost the lad I love,
    But I'll dry these selfish tears,
For this swain of mine is gone to join
    The British volunteers.
And where's a maiden in the land,
    With soul so cold and mean,
That would not part with the lad of her heart
    In the service of the Queen.

CHORUS.

    Then sound the trumpet, beat the drum,
        And let us give nine cheers
    For each brave soul in the muster roll
        Of the British Volunteers.

And when at length he shall return,
    And these dreadful wars are o'er,
I shall sit by his side a smiling bride,
    And he'll wander forth no more.
How proud of my good man I'll be,
    When the neighbours flock to hear
Of the brave deeds done, and the battles won,
    By the British Volunteer.
        Then sound the trumpet, &c.

In quietude we'll end our days,
    In some nice pleasant cot,
On the glory that my hero's gained,
    And the money he has got;
And when at last his hair turns grey,
    I'll cherish my old dear,
And I'll think of the time when he fought in his prime,
    As a British Volunteer.
            Then sound the trumpet, &c.

Put your Shoulder to the Wheel.

[Set to Music by George Simpson, and published by Messrs. D'Almaine
and Co., 20, Soho Square, London, to whom the Copyright belongs.]

They tell us times are very bad, they say there's great
    distress,
But think ye that to talk about will ever make it less;
Oh, no! 'twere far the better plan, the wiser course a deal,
To leave off grumbling, and to put your shoulder to tho
    wheel.
Few evils that this country knows but what would soon
    give place,
If men would only calmly meet and look them in the face;
Self brought about, as I contend, they are, there's little doubt
That we who caus'd their growth possess the power to put
    them out.

CHORUS.

Then up at once, and to the task, no longer idly sit
Waiting till greater folks begin, the least can help a bit,
Let high and low together go, what Englishman would
    pause,
Throughout the land to lend a hand and work in such
    a cause ;
There's not a wound in England found but what her sons
    can heal,
And all that's wanted is to put your shoulder to the wheel.

Extravagance (nay do not frown), extravagance, I say,
Among us all too long hath held its deleterious sway,
Let each adopt this golden rule, which yet may pull us
    through,
If little be our comings in, to make that little do,
Like clever mariners at sea, who, on their voyage you'll find,
Take in their sails, or crowd each spar according to the wind ;
This is the secret of success, the cure of all our woes,
And God forbid old England's sons should prove old England's
    foes.

    Then up at once, and to the task, no longer idly sit, &c.

A very High Pressure Empromptu.

DEAREST Miss REED, once the Graces agreed,
    To surpass all they ever had done,
So each lent her aid in bedecking a maid,
    And, loveliest, thou art that one!

The Widowed Bird.

THE grove is silent, and alone is heard
The pious mourning of a widowed bird,
Who weeps unceasingly her mate at rest,
Her offspring nestled to her throbbing breast.
O'erwhelmed in woe, her faithful heart she steeps
In sorrow's font, and mournful vigil keeps,
Becoming grief.   Yet, certain seasons past,
It is decreed the dark hour may not last.
The heart's warm blood, with gentle joy elate,
At Nature's bidding, asks another mate ;
(Wise dispensation for the common good—
A feeling never to be long withstood).
Love lives on memory till time-soften'd hours
Into another source its fondness pours.
Soon as the feather'd choir began to sing
Their hymn of gratitude to welcome Spring,
Each innate feeling, thus by music stirr'd,
Its genial influence reached the Widowed Bird.
Unerring Nature wills that every kind,
Alike in feeling, character and mind,
Consort together, and neglecting this,
Small, small indeed, the chance of wedded bliss.
The lovely Philomel, with instinct rife,
Takes none save Nightingale to be his wife :
Thrush will to Thrush, as Lark to Lark repairs,
From fellow feeling known each other's cares ;

Each joy divided, and each sorrow known,
And met with kindred feeling all its own.
Thus time wore on, as yet no bird had come
Congenial partner of her heart and home.
A dreary void her " bosom's lord " besets,
A life is hers of sighs and vain regrets ;
At last, in happy hour, one draweth near,
Whose warbled notes fall sweetly on her ear,
With fluttering plumage, see he gains her side,
And once again the Widowed Bird's a bride.

Impromptu.

[On a young lady's expressing her intention of marrying a gentleman,
who she herself confessed had few qualifications beyond the possession
of four hundred and fifty pounds per annum.]

ANY young man, good-looking, whose income is clear
Four hundred and fifty pounds sterling a year,
May address the fair Charlotte without any fear,
But he must have four hundred and fifty a year.

She says, and methinks the assertion sounds queer,
All depends on four hundred and fifty a year,
That if a large family folks are to rear,
It makes a hole in four hundred and fifty a year.

Says, few joys are by Providence granted us here,
But grow out of four hundred and fifty a year,
That connubial orisons at all times are clear,
If backed by four hundred and fifty a year.

That the heart's warmest throb, or affection's fond tear
Are as nought to four hundred and fifty a year ;
Through the ocean of life no fond couple can steer
Save the freight is four hundred and fifty a year.

Now, I rather imagine a woman's heart dear
That is bought by four hundred and fifty a year ;
Possessors of incomes, I pray you don't see her,
Or God help your four hundreds and fifties a year.

Yet, faith ! I'll be candid, take courage ; draw near—
She's well worth four hundred and fifty a year :
I love her myself, but I cannot tell where
To get hold of four hundred and fifty a year.

So my chance is over, as things now appear,
And all through four hundred and fifty a year !
Still heaven await her ; tho', mind you, Up There
They heed not four hundreds and fifties a year.

Additional Verse to the National Anthem.

And when in Freedom's cause
England's bright Sword she draws,
    O grant Thine aid ;
On each dread battle field
Make her proud foemen yield ;
Be thou her help and shield :
    God save the Queen.

PRINTED BY BEMROSE & SONS, DERBY.

www.ingramcontent.com/pod-product-compliance
Lightning Source LLC
Chambersburg PA
CBHW030901050726
47500CB00009B/863